sitting shiva

sitting shiva

a novel by

elliot feldman

illustrations by elliot feldman

foxrock books
•new york•

To Cathie for her encouragement
To John Rechy for his guidance
To the memory of Abe Feldman
and Dr. Charles McCammon

"SHIVA," (SHIV'A), is the Hebrew word for "seven." In Judaism, it refers to the seven-day mourning period that begins immediately after a funeral and is observed at the home of the deceased. The Jewish custom of mourning for seven days is based on the verse in Genesis where Joseph mourns his father Jacob for a week. "Sitting shiva" refers to the low stools customarily used during this period of mourning. These seven intense days help survivors face the reality of a loved one's death, and help them move from mourning to living.

the funeral

· 1976 ·

AN HOUR BEFORE the funeral service, Charlie Fish couldn't think of one thing to say about his father.

In the mahogany-paneled rabbi's office at the City Of David Mortuary, the door opened a crack and Rabbi Benjamin Schwarz poked his Wally Walrus face into the room. His shaggy eyebrows raised with hopeful expectation. "Are you almost ready with your speech, Mr. Fish?" His voice was a tentative squeak.

"Maybe I should forget about it, Rabbi," Charlie stammered.

"You really should say something, Mr. Fish. I'll give you more time." The office door shut with a polite impatient snap.

Charlie stared at the blank sheet of paper on the rabbi's desk, a ball-point pen clutched in his sweating hand. With his other hand, he nervously rubbed his chest-length curly black beard. He hated his father's natty black mohair suit. It clashed with Charlie's scruffy demeanor. It was several sizes too big for him, and too heavy for the humid ninety-degree Michigan August day. He had no suits of his own, other than a patchwork Levi blue jean jacket and matching pants. His mother urged him to wear his father's suit, which was bought only a month before his death.

Charlie began to write. "Morris Fish was . . ."

He stopped writing.

Morris Fish was *what*?

A wave of unexplainable anger hit him. He finished the sentence. "Morris Fish was a fuck-up, a liar, a bully, a weak man with uncontrollable vices. "

He closed his eyes and could see his father's face: Morris Fish at 40 years old, in his prime; a face purple with rage; a flattened boxer's nose accentuating his brutality; a cursing mouth baring stubby brown cigarette-stained teeth. This face scared the shit out of Charlie, a face that he remembered from his teen years. The face of "the bad Morris Fish." Charlie's eyes jolted open, a queasy pain in his belly.

He quickly scribbled more words on the page. "Morris Fish was full of shit. He was never around when I was growing up. He was either hiding out from creditors, especially Lowell Krantz. He shacked up with whores, played cards with mobsters and millionaires, or slept it all off on my mother's goddamn pride and joy plastic-covered living room couch. Morris Fish was a degenerate gambler."

He crumpled up the page and tossed it in the wastebasket.

He pressed his face against the rabbi's desk. He tried to think about "the good Morris Fish," the handsome face with the perpetual beard stubble, the close-cropped curly salt-and-pepper hair, and the Clark Gable mustache.

"Morris Fish had the gift of gab. He was a charmer," he wrote.

Charlie snarled and ripped up the page into tiny pieces. He rubbed his fists into his eyes. He scribbled on a new piece of paper . . .

"Who was Morris Fish? Who the hell am I?"

∴

· 1959 ·

FROM SECOND TO fifth grade, Charlie was the class clown. He made everyone laugh, including the teachers. His ready quips and especially his obscure impressions of Walter Brennan, Dennis Weaver, and Ed Wynn made him the center of attention.

In private, among his many fifth grade pals, his showstopper imitation was Goofy screwing Daisy Duck. He did both voices.

A series of open-minded second- to fifth-grade teachers saw his sense of humor as a rare talent. They allowed his creativity to run free in the classroom, especially Mrs. Smather, his fifth-grade teacher. For her class, Charlie was allowed to do a scene of Shakespeare's "Hamlet," giving the characters a variety of Yiddish accents. He called his version "Hemlet Mit Eggs."

"To be or not to be. Dot iss a qvestion?!"

Charlie's fun came to a halt in sixth grade, when he was transferred to a newly constructed school, Dewey Elementary.

Mrs. Lipkis, his sixth grade teacher, wasn't a fan of his humor; particularly when he "became Elvis" for a whole day, wearing wraparound shades, scotch-taping Kleenex sideburns to his cheeks, and answering all questions in mono-syllables: "yes'm" and "no'm," punctuated with an occasional lip-sneer and "uh-huh-uh-huh-uh-huh." His classmates laughed loud.

Charlie was relentless. On other days he became other characters: "Bond—James Bond," "Nyah-ha-ha" Snidely

Whiplash, "Godfrey Daniel" W.C. Fields. For every disruption, Mrs. Lipkis would send him to the office of the vice-principal, Dr. Artunian, who would then call Charlie's mother, Celia Fish. This scenario played out at least twice a week during the first few months of sixth grade at Dewey School.

Celia was horrified to discover that her son was a "discipline problem." She never understood his humor and his crudely drawn comics. Celia's sense of humor was simple at best. She could only understand the broadest slapstick.

Charlie's "nutty actions" and "foolish jokes" terrified her. Above all, she hated her son's cartoon drawings, his demented Mad Magazine-style characters with their popping eyeballs, slavering tongues, and feverish beads of sweat. She encouraged him to draw happy fuzzy animals like the ones that populated Walt Disney's "Bambi." Charlie's creatures horrified her.

He had no trouble making his father laugh. Morris Fish understood Charlie's sense of humor. He had his own word for Charlie's humor: "worbid"—a combination of "warped" and "morbid".

After vice-principal Artunian warned Charlie's parents about his "behavior problem," they cracked down on him, peeling back his TV watching time to one hour a week. To Charlie, this punishment was almost a death sentence. Television was his ultimate escape. He toned down his class clown routine; his war on Dewey Elementary became much subtler. His verbal disruptions ended and he began drawing vulgar caricatures of teachers: Mr. Vandegraff the counselor and his constantly unzipped fly; Miss Merkle the librarian and her lipstick-smeared teeth; and he drew Mrs. Lipkis as a rabid bulldog foaming at the mouth.

He passed these comics to his classmates. They roared with laughter, especially the hoods.

In mid-term, his sixth grade life exploded when Mrs. Lipkis discovered one of his more vulgar comics inside his classroom desk drawer. In the drawing, Mrs. Lipkis, vice-principal Artunian, Mrs. McGurk the mannish girls' gym teacher, and several other Dewey teachers were engaged in a nude doggie-style daisy chain.

Mrs. Lipkis marched Charlie to the principal's office. He was suspended on the spot and sent home.

His walk home was slow and painful. His head throbbed with a stress migraine. The ache was so intense, he could see nothing but a mass of bright throbbing electric-yellow spots.

He dragged past Westridge Street's nearly identical modest aluminum-sided houses. His house was on the corner of Westridge and Granzon. His parents' car was parked in the driveway. It was unusual that they were both home at two in the afternoon.

Charlie opened the screen door with its aluminum "F" for Fish.

His father was sitting on the plastic-covered couch in the living room. His mother sat next to the couch, thin and frail in her wheelchair. Although she could walk, it took too much exertion to do so. She needed a wheelchair.

"Charles, we just received a call from Dr. Artunian, your

vice-principal." Celia Fish's voice cracked with emotion. Her bright orange perfect Lucille Ball-style bouffant-bubble hairdo trembled.

Migraine pain shot through Charlie's eyeballs. He hated his mother's dramatics.

Celia Fish had been an invalid most of her life, surviving ten years in a tuberculosis sanitorium, Herman Kiefer Hospital. Charlie was born there.

"Dr. Artunian suggested that you see a child psychologist. I've made an appointment for you." Celia Fish's body wracked with sobs.

"What the hell's the matter with you, kid?" growled Morris Fish.

"Your father and I are ashamed, damn you! I'm ashamed. No one on either side of the family has ever seen a psychiatrist, but we have no choice. You're *abnormal!*" she screamed.

To Celia Fish, being "abnormal" was the ultimate sin. As a teenager, Celia didn't fit in. She was sickly and only four feet nine inches tall. The other girls called her "the eighth dwarf." She wanted Charlie to fit in.

Morris Fish stared at his son and shook his head in disgust.

Charlie had heard this conversation many times before.

"I don't feel so good." He turned to leave the room.

"Don't you walk away from us. We're talking to you," his mother sobbed.

"I'm onto you, kid. Don't think I ain't. You an' your headaches. You're fakin' it, aren't ya?" growled Morris Fish.

sitting shiva

Charlie felt faint, bumped against the wall, then staggered to his bedroom.

∵

THE child psychologist's office was in the converted garage of a stylish ranch home in a residential area of Royal Oak.

Dr. Dalrymple was a dreary old woman with permanently pursed lips, horn-rimmed glasses, and crepe-soled sensible shoes.

Although Charlie's inventive interpretations of the Rorschach ink blots—particularly the "elephant kissing a ballerina"—gave the psychologist pause, she assured Celia and Morris Fish that their son was a "normal yet creative boy, but his creativity is causing disruptive behavior in the classroom." The doctor recommended that both parents actively encourage their son's creativity "outside the classroom." That Celia should enroll him in private art lessons at the Detroit Institute of Art downtown, that Morris should take him to "sporting events," and that they should invite "more gregarious" neighborhood boys over for lunches.

The psychologist's parting words were a warning that if Charlie's disruptive behavior continued, vice-principal Artunian wouldn't hesitate to put him in "a special class for the emotionally disturbed."

These words alarmed Charlie. He knew that hoods "pounded" the "special ed" kids on a daily basis.

Charlie's classroom personality changed because he had

no choice. To bait him, Mrs. Lipkis would toss out comedy straight-lines, and he wouldn't respond. Charlie wouldn't joke with anyone. In class, his sense of humor was not only stifled, it was gone.

For years, his jokes and his one and only friend, Joe Murphy, kept the hoods from stomping him every day.

At six feet four inches tall, Joe was the largest and toughest hood in the neighborhood. Charlie and Joe became friends because of a shared interest in collecting movie monster magazines and drawing comics. Every day they'd either meet at the comic book rack at Hammerstein's drugstore, or behind the old one-room schoolhouse to ogle a Playboy magazine that Charlie had filched from his father's underwear drawer.

Unfortunately, when Charlie was transferred to Dewey Elementary, Joe wasn't there to save his ass. Like nearly half of the kids in Oak Park, Joe Murphy's parents had decided to send him to Our Lady of Mercy Catholic school instead of public school.

At Dewey, Charlie's worst fears were realized. He still became a "target," even though he wasn't one of the special ed kids.

⁖

WALKING home from the new school, Charlie took his usual route, crossing Nine Mile Road and heading toward the Eagle Dairy, home of his favorite chocolate malt and hangout of the more vicious local hoods.

Charlie's stomach churned upon seeing Chris Korkis and David Rothman, his archenemies, leaning against the Eagle's front window. Unfiltered Kools dangled from their lips.

David Rothman was a mean-eyed runt with Elvis Presley hair, and Chris Korkis was his two-hundred-pound, six-foot-tall enforcer. They were cutting school.

"Hey, Brillo!" sneered Korkis's flat gravelly voice.

They called Charlie "Brillo" because of his wild shock of black kinky hair, a physical attribute that he shared with his father. Charlie lowered his head, aimed his eyes at the sidewalk, and walked quickly past them, pretending not to hear.

They never hassled him when Joe Murphy was around. Charlie was fair game when caught alone.

Korkis and Rothman hated him for years—since the day that he singlehandedly lost the Little League city baseball championship for the Busy Bee Hardware Stingers team. Charlie had dropped an easy right-field pop fly, allowing the winning run to score.

His participation in Little League was only due to his mother's relentless campaign to make him into a "normal boy."

"Whatsamatter, Brillo? You deaf as well as dumb?" chuckled Rothman's high-pitched nasal voice.

Charlie stuffed down his rage and kept walking.

Korkis walked after him and connected with a swift kick in his ass. Charlie lurched forward but didn't fall.

"Puck puck! Chicken Brillo!" shouted Chris Korkis.

Charlie kept walking and turned down Westridge Avenue.

He could still hear Rothman's laughter, a jackass's bray.

⁘

INSTEAD of taking Charlie to "sporting events," as Dr. Dalrymple recommended, Morris had an unorthodox solution. He bought a regulation-sized pool table for the knotty-pine-finished basement of the Oak Park home.

To his own surprise, Charlie enjoyed his father's gift. Stroking the table's smooth dark wood and the soft lush green felt was a pleasurable experience for him. He liked the challenge of shooting the brightly colored balls into the side pockets.

For the first time in Charlie's life, Morris Fish spent time with him every day. For a month, his father taught him the finer points of the game: how to use the bridge, how to bank the cueball, how to do a behind-the-back shot.

Morris Fish even stayed home from his daily card game to play pool with his son. They talked. They swapped sick jokes and groaned.

"What's the difference between a bowling ball and a dead baby?"

"I dunno."

"You can't load a bowling ball onto the back of a truck with a pitchfork."

For the first time, Morris and Charlie were a real father and son team, and Charlie was getting good at the game of pool.

The closeness with his father came to an abrupt end when Celia started to feel that the time Charlie spent with his father was "unhealthy." She believed that he needed to be around boys his own age. She spread the word around the neighborhood about the new pool table.

David Rothman and Chris Korkis were among the first boys to show up. Celia Fish considered these two to be "normal red blooded kids." To her, any boy that played baseball was a "normal red blooded kid."

Soon Charlie's basement was teeming with newfound "friends." Even when he wasn't home, the basement would be full of kids. Celia was thrilled to bake trays of cookies for these boys.

Celia and Morris Fish were convinced that their son was on his way toward normalcy. Charlie was beginning to believe that he had regained his lost popularity. In the privacy of his parents' basement, he could crack as many jokes as he wanted. He could even say "shit," "fuck," and "fart" as many times as he wanted, and at the top of his lungs.

Joe Murphy acted as "sergeant-of-arms," tossing out any boy who didn't treat Charlie or Charlie's basement with the proper respect. Above all, Joe made sure that there was no gambling.

The good times ended when one of Joe Murphy's more tasteless jokes fizzled in Celia Fish's face. In full view of the Fish family at dinnertime, Joe ate a tuna biscuit from Charlie's dog Susie's dish.

Celia banned him from the Fish house. Charlie was no longer allowed to hang out with him. She even paid Korkis and Rothman a dollar a day to be her "spies," making sure that Charlie stayed far away from Joe Murphy.

Charlie and Joe still had their secret meeting place behind the old one-room schoolhouse. They met there every day to swap monster magazines, comic books, and lewd stories.

With Joe Murphy no longer present as "pool table enforcer," Charlie's basement became Korkis and Rothman's basement. His pool table became their pool table. They began taking bets on games. They used Charlie's father's poker chips as a cover. Celia and even Morris thought that they were playing for fun. Neighborhood kids would buy chips with their newspaper route, grocery store bagboy, and restaurant busboy wages. Rothman and Korkis were "the house."

Every day the basement was filled with young gamblers. Rothman and Korkis began taking IOUs.

Howie Schultz, a tiny orthodox Jewish kid with curly sidelocks and a gambling problem, owed them $100. One day they dragged the much smaller boy into Charlie's basement laundry room, stuffed him inside Celia Fish's clothes dryer, and turned it on.

Charlie grabbed a pool cue, raised it in a threatening gesture, and threatened to tell his father, who was sleeping upstairs. "Get outta my house!" he shouted.

Chris Korkis laughed. He was much larger than Charlie.

David Rothman sneered, "Screw you, Fish. Do you think we're here because we like you? You're a goddamn joke. A goddamn nothing with a pool table. Nobody really likes you, Fish. Your old man ain't worth a shit either. My parents say so. He's just a low-life gambler, a Mafia bagman."

Charlie screamed with rage and swung the pool cue at David Rothman's head.

Chris Korkis seized Charlie's arm and twisted it until he dropped the cuestick.

As Korkis slammed him against a knotty pine paneled wall, little Howie Schultz scrambled out of the clothes dryer and ran for his life.

Charlie tried to kick and squirm out of Korkis's grasp. The bigger boy pinned him harder against the wall.

"Never interfere with our private business, Fish!" David Rothman growled as he slammed his fist into Charlie's gut.

Charlie gasped and sagged to the cold cement of the basement laundry room floor.

Korkis and Rothman laughed and walked back into the crowded smoke-filled poolroom. They resumed their game. Players stacked their chips on the table.

Charlie was a stranger in his own house.

Rage filled him. His head and gut hurt. He scrambled to his feet. He staggered into the pool table room.

To relieve the pain and humiliation, he screamed at the top of his lungs. "Fuck you! Fuck all of you!"

"Look at the cry-baby," chuckled David Rothman. Chris Korkis laughed and raked in five-dollar chips. The other boys ignored Charlie, and the game of rotation pool continued.

Charlie ran out of his house, leaving full reign of the basement to his worst enemies.

He ran across the street and through the Pyzbylskis' back yard, hopped their fence, and landed flat on his ass on the Arthur Vandenburg Junior High playground.

"Hey, Gefilte Fish! You have a nice trip?" chuckled a jolly sandpaper voice that should've belonged to an old man instead of fourteen-year-old Joe Murphy. He was sitting on top of a playground slide smoking a Pall Mall, his thick lips twisted in a goofball grin.

Charlie's anger dissipated upon seeing his good buddy. "What's happening, Frankenstein?"

Joe and Charlie were an unlikely pair. Charlie was short, round, and sardonic. Joe was a hulking redhead with a raucous sense of humor and a dopey good-natured grin.

Joe's vulgar artwork, particularly his trademark bareboobed blondes, could be found on storefronts and men's rooms all over Oak Park. This didn't put him in good stead with local merchants and the Oak Park police.

"Look what I got, Charlie." Joe proudly displayed a full-unopened jumbo box of Crayolas. "All the colors of the rainbow. I boosted it from the Ben Franklin."

Charlie laughed and applauded. "The infamous sticky fingers of Frankenstein strike again!"

They walked to a far corner of the playground, to the old one-room schoolhouse. The hundred-year-old tiny clapboard building was no longer in use. It was dwarfed by the recently constructed Vandenburg Junior High. The Oak Park city fathers decided to keep the old schoolhouse as a historical site. Although Charlie and Joe Murphy both attended kindergarten in the schoolhouse, neither one felt any sentimentality toward it.

Joe opened the box of Crayolas and the two boys went to work on the whitewashed walls. They drew werewolves clutching severed heads, vampires with bloody fangs, hollow-eyed mummies, and buck-naked Hollywood scream queens.

The whoop of a police car siren interrupted their fun. Borlack, a burly town cop with a trademark handlebar mustache, grabbed the boys by their shirt collars and hauled them off to the Oak Park police station, his siren blaring for maximum effect.

Celia and Morris Fish came to the police station to bail Charlie out.

"I—I'm sorry," he stammered to his parents. His father folded his arms across his chest and turned his back on him. Celia burst into tears and hurled one word at her son.

"Abnormal!"

The next day, Morris bought a canvas tarp and covered the pool table. All the neighborhood kids, including Rothman and Korkis, were turned away at the front door. Rothman, Korkis, and the other hoods turned the screws on Charlie harder than before. The word "Crybaby!" was painted across his school locker door, his textbooks were glued together, and his cafeteria lunches were snatched. The hoods, above all, would verbally humiliate him in front of girls, particularly Judy Weinstein . . . beautiful Judy Weinstein with her shiny black hair, alabaster skin, and bright blue eyes.

Judy Weinstein laughed at Charlie's jokes and admired his drawings. She was the only girl who appreciated him. It killed Charlie to be tortured in front of Judy Weinstein.

School became a bleeding hell for him.

At home, his mother would look at him and burst into violent wracking sobs. Morris Fish wouldn't speak to him.

Charlie never again touched the pool table. The tarp gave the table an eerie ghostlike appearance.

Real and imagined physical symptoms began to plague Charlie daily: throbbing migraines, wheezing allergies, and red oozing acne and boils covering all parts of his body. It was hard for him to believe that he was once called Celia Fish's "miracle baby."

• Yom Kippur, 1948 •

NO ONE THOUGHT that Celia was strong enough to survive the ordeal of childbirth, but she did. At almost two years old, Charlie was an adorable child.

Little Charlie was all pudge, dimples, and bright brown eyes with a thatch of black hair molded into a large jellyroll curl on the top of his head.

For the first five years of his life, Morris Fish raised Charlie while his mother was in the hospital. During those years Morris became his father and his mother.

Little Charlie was slow to speak. When he did speak, it was in one word sentences: "Doggie," "Birdy," "Hi," "Bye," and "No."

This was Charlie's second Yom Kippur dinner at his Aunt Beatrice's house. As the newest family baby, he was the center of attention.

At the Yom Kippur dinner, Charlie and his father were given seats of honor near Aunt Beatrice, Uncle Sheldon, Grandpa Aaron, and Grandma Rifka. Family members set aside all prior differences with Morris Fish and lavished their love and praises on little Charlie.

Charlie was especially adorable this evening, clad in a full cowboy suit, climbing nonstop over chairs and couches in Aunt Beatrice's living room, firing his brand-new Hopalong Cassidy cap gun at chuckling relatives, squealing with delight and shouting "Bank! Bank! Bank! Bank!" at the top of his lungs.

His father yanked the cap gun out of his hand. With a mean smile, Morris clutched the gun tightly to his chest and shouted "Mine!"

The game began.

"No, mine!" little Charlie screamed back.

The relatives laughed at these antics, not immediately seeing the underlying cruelty.

"No! It's miiiine!" Morris shouted back at him, clutching the gun even tighter to his chest.

The relatives howled as the baby reached desperately at the toy gun in his father's hands. Charlie's eyes filled with tears.

"Look at him. Look. He's fighting back. He's just like his old man, except his old man never cried," Morris Fish guffawed.

"Enough already, Morris! Give him back the gun," snarled Grandma Rifka.

"No. He's gonna have to take it from me. I'm teachin' him one of life's lessons."

Charlie cried loudly as he beat on his father's hands with both fists.

"Whatsamatter? 'You a little crying baby? . . . C'mon! Take it away from me!" mocked his father.

Charlie screamed in rage and dug his fingernails into his father's hands.

The relatives were no longer laughing.

"Look. The little *pisher* thinks he's Rocky Marciano. C'mon. Give your old man a belt," chuckled Morris.

"*Genug*, Morris! Enough!" shouted Grandma Rifka.

"Okay. Okay, *boychick*," Morris chuckled and handed the gun to Charlie. "Here's your *farshtunkiner* gun."

"Mine!" the boy yelled defiantly, clutching the toy gun to his chest and sobbing.

"Yeah, kid. It's yours," laughed Morris.

Charlie bellowed with rage and hit his father with the butt of the gun, splitting his eyebrow with a loud metallic clack.

Morris jolted as a thin trickle of blood ran down into his

right eye. His face twisted into an angry grimace. He grabbed Charlie's arm.

The relatives gasped. They had all been on the receiving end of Morris Fish's violent temper.

"No, Morris!" screamed Grandma Rifka, as he pulled Charlie across the living room.

The boy yelled and kicked as Morris dragged him out of the house.

He picked up the crying boy, slung him over his shoulder like a dufflebag, and headed to the brand new black Hudson Hornet.

"I'll teach you to hit me. I'm gonna spank you upside-down an' you'll never forget it!" Morris flung open the car's rear door and dropped Charlie inside.

He climbed in after the boy, shut the car door, and locked it. Morris stared coldly at his son. "You little shit, nobody makes me bleed."

Charlie screamed in terror and kicked at his father. Morris snatched him by the ankles with one beefy hand and pulled him to an upside-down position. The little boy wiggled and squirmed helplessly in his father's grip.

"Now I'll learn ya!" Morris cracked his son's ass with his free hand.

Charlie stopped crying.

His father hit him harder.

Charlie didn't utter a sound.

Morris spun the boy around. Charlie glared at his father.

Morris Fish bellowed with unexpected laughter. "So, you little shit, you really do got balls, don't ya?"

He dropped the boy. Charlie landed on the car seat.

"How about we go to Eagle Dairy for some ice cream?" he chuckled.

This offer didn't quell Charlie's fury.

"Don't stare at me like that, kid. Some day you'll thank me for this."

• 1976 •

THE CITY OF David Chapel looked like a converted high school auditorium embellished with stained glass window scenes that looked more like Classics Illustrated "Greatest Moments from the Bible" comics.

The room was packed with mourners, most making amends for deserting Morris Fish in his declining years.

Rabbi Schwarz addressed them from a podium at the front of the stage. Charlie sat behind him in an uncomfortable heavy wooden chair. His sweaty forehead could be blamed more on stage fright than heat. He stared down at his shoes, afraid to look into the audience.

He could only hear the solemn droning sound of the rabbi's voice, not the words. The words meant nothing to him. Rabbi Schwarz had never met Morris Fish.

This is bullshit, thought Charlie. My father was a Jew who wouldn't enter a synagogue. He was a Jew who was never bar-mitzvahed.

He remembered his father's Hebrew school story.

At age 12, Morris Fish was expelled after a one-punch

knockout of his religious teacher, a fierce autocratic ex-captain in the Russian army who still carried a rawhide officer's whipping stick for discipline. This one-punch knockout created Morris Fish's personal legend, "the Jew who wouldn't take shit," and sealed his father's fate forever as the black sheep of the Fish family. The un-bar-mitzvahed son.

As Charlie grew up, he became "the black sheep son of the black sheep."

Rabbi Schwarz's speech presented a different Morris Fish legend. "He was a perfect husband, a devoted son, a caring brother, and a war hero." Charlie heard these words and knew that they came directly from his Aunt Beatrice Fish Sternbaum.

He felt anger.

"Charles Fish would now like to say a few words about his father." Rabbi Schwarz turned toward Charlie with a small tense smile.

Charlie stood up. He felt lightheaded. He wobbled a bit and held onto the chair's arm. He gathered his courage and stared out at the many faces in the crowded chapel. He could recognize only about ten of these faces, and could focus only on his mother.

She was the center of attention, a tiny crumpled figure in her wheelchair. Friends and relatives surrounded her, leaning close, stroking her shoulders and hands, whispering words of support. Being a widow suited her. Charlie knew that she enjoyed being the center of attention.

He walked with uneasy steps to the *bima*. His fists nervously clenched and unclenched. He jammed them into the pockets of the black mohair suit jacket. Rabbi Schwarz's shaggy eyebrows knotted together in a worried expression as he yielded the microphone to Charlie.

The last time he spoke in front of a crowd of strangers was at his bar mitzvah.

• 1960 •

CHARLIE FISH'S BAR MITZVAH was Oak Park's party of the year. Celia Fish had transformed the cavernous and stark banquet room of Sol's Restaurant into a temporary Shangri-La with table linen and bunting in shades of baby-boy-blue. She invited three hundred guests—everyone she knew, including fair-weather friends, newfound acquaintances, and long-lost twelfth cousins.

She hired Billy Friedkin's Orchestra of Distinction, a popular purveyor of foxtrots, Jewish *hora* music, and Latin syncopation with "the featured cha cha and meringue dance stylings of Enrique and Silvia," whose real names were Elvin and Betty Sue Dismukes.

Celia had also hired Arnie Boston, Detroit's top party photographer. He took color movies and still photos of the affair for "the bar mitzvah photo book to end all bar mitzvah photo books."

Sol Shribman, owner and head chef of Sol's Restaurant, created a "three course banquet extraordinaire" for Celia, his Cornish game hen stuffed with wild rice as "the piece de resistance."

To Charlie, the party was a farce. In all of the excitement, he was almost forgotten. His best friend Joe Murphy wasn't even invited. His mother wanted to invite David Rothman and Chris Korkis, but Charlie would rather have no kids invited than those two snakes.

Morris Fish was at the open bar, slowly getting sloshed on Four Roses whiskey to deaden the painful bite that this party would take out of his wallet.

The bar mitzvah was the crowning moment of Celia Fish's life, but it had very little relevance to Charlie Fish's ascent into manhood.

The lavish affair was Celia's vindication for all the years spent in the tuberculosis sanitorium. She would frequently tell Charlie about all the years without friends and family at her bedside. She would talk about being the only Jew in a hospital ward packed with coughing and dying working-class Polish and Irish Catholics who had never known a Jew.

The party told the world that she had not only survived, but flourished. Tears of joy rolled down Celia Fish's face. This was the one and only time that Charlie had ever seen his mother experiencing a state of near-total happiness.

He watched his father on the dance floor. He was dancing a slow drunken belly-rubbing foxtrot with Dorothy Pevsner, a stacked redheaded divorced woman with a bad facelift. Morris Fish was snickering into her ear. Mrs. Pevsner was blushing and giggling. Charlie knew what his father was saying. He was either already fucking her or planning to fuck her. Throughout the years, Charlie had overheard his father bragging to his poker cronies about his many "pieces of ass."

sitting shiva

He hated his father for betraying his mother. He hated his father's vulgar foxtrot on the dance floor at his bar mitzvah party.

Celia kept busy, wheeling herself from guest to guest. She ignored Morris's shenanigans. It wasn't important to her.

Charlie felt physically ill. He searched for a hiding place. He entered the coatroom and closed the door.

When it was time for the candle-lighting ceremony, Aunt Beatrice found Charlie's hiding place and ordered him into the limelight at the front of the bandstand.

Sol Schribman's multitiered rum cream cake was wheeled out on a cart. A bride and groom should have been on the top tier instead of thirteen birthday candles; however, for Celia, the dramatic effect was all that mattered. She had carefully choreographed the candle-lighting ceremony, the central event of the evening.

The "most important people" in Celia Fish's life would light Charlie's thirteen birthday candles. In reverse pecking order, the candle lighting would start with immediate family members from the Fish-Sternbaum side, then continue with members of Celia's Nosanchuk side of the family. The last candle-lighters would be Celia and Morris Fish.

Orchestra leader Billy Friedkin was master of ceremonies, doing his best Jewish Cab Calloway hipster impression, decked out in an iridescent green tux with tails, his dark hair pomaded straight back. Friedkin stood in front of the cake, his microphone in one hand and thirteen index cards in the other hand. Each card had a short, too-gracious tribute to each candle-lighter, written in Celia Fish's distinctive flowery curlicue handwriting style

The bar mitzvah boy stood stiffly next to Friedkin, a painful smile frozen on his face as the procession of Fishes and Nosanchuks lit each candle. He shook hands and hugged relatives. His face was smeared with a variety of stinky lipsticks.

Celia beamed as she clutched the long lighting-candle, the thirteenth candle, for the evening's climax. She was as radiant as a queen, her wheelchair a rolling throne.

Morris stood next to her, red-faced and roaring drunk. He moved close to Charlie.

"Today you are a man, *boychick!*" he guffawed, then roughly grabbed his son's face with both hands. Charlie's eyes widened with fear. He could smell his father's whiskey and El Producto cigar breath. His stomach turned.

He tried to jerk away from his father, but Morris pulled him closer and kissed him full on the mouth. The crowd laughed and applauded. Celia blushed with good-natured embarrassment.

Charlie felt rage and nausea within him. He pushed his father in the chest as hard as he could, breaking the kiss.

His father's face twisted into an expression of hurt and humiliation. The audience laughter and applause faded to silence.

His mother grabbed Charlie's arm and pulled him down to her eye level. "Apologize to your father," she growled into Charlie's ear.

"No!" He jerked his arm out of her grasp.

Arnie Boston captured the whole scene on film. After a dirty look from Celia, he turned off the camera.

Billy Friedkin cued his band to quietly play "Everything's Coming Up Roses," a practiced emergency ploy for embarrassing party moments.

Celia turned her wheelchair away from the crowd. She faced her son. "You're not only abnormal, you're a betrayer! You ruined everything!" The music drowned out her screaming voice.

Morris tried to comfort Celia to no avail.

"You shut up, too!" she shrieked at Morris.

He shook his head in disgust, and walked back to the bar.

Charlie ran for the Sol's Restaurant mensroom. He hunched over a toilet bowl and puked out Cornish game hen and wild rice.

For weeks after the bar mitzvah, his father refused to speak to him, and his mother couldn't look at him without bursting into tears. To Celia, her son had stolen her one perfect moment.

She would have one more perfect moment in her life: her husband's funeral.

• 1976 •

RABBI SCHWARZ IMPATIENTLY cleared his throat. Charlie had been silent at the podium for several minutes. He tried to speak, but the words wouldn't come. He nervously fingered a small right inner pocket of the suit jacket. A hard flat object was inside the pocket.

He removed a plastic comb. Morris Fish's plastic comb. He stared down at it. Kinky gray and black hair were clumped in the comb's teeth.

His father's hair.

A wave of deep sadness washed over him. He saw his father's laughing face. He could hear Morris Fish's deep belly laugh inside his head. Only Charlie could make his father laugh like that. He liked his father's laughter.

The sound of the laughter faded, replaced by Eddie Fisher's voice singing "Oh My Papa."

He hated this syrupy song. It was Morris Fish's favorite song.

He hated and loved his father.

Tears poured from Charlie's eyes.

He began to speak. No, he began to *sing*.

"Oh, my papa. To me, he was so wonderful . . ."

•••

AFTER the memorial service, Morris Fish's body was transported thirty miles away to the Workmen's Circle Cemetery near Mount Clemens, where two generations of Nosanchuks, Celia's family, were buried.

Workmen's Circle, an immigrant Hebrew socialist benevolent society, established the cemetery around the time of the Great War. Despite its historical significance as Detroit's oldest Jewish cemetery, Workmen's Circle was an ugly place. Upright cracked granite headstones were crowded together and leaned at irregular angles. Most of the headstones had hand-carved Hebrew words of love and devotion. On some of the headstones, imbedded glass bubbles encased faded photographs of the deceased. Weeds and dandelions grew wild between the headstones.

Charlie wanted his father buried in the roomier and newer Machpelach Cemetery near the Michigan State Fairgrounds. Two generations of Fishes and Gelbfisczes, the family's pre-Ellis Island name, were buried at Machpelach, but his mother insisted on abiding by Nosanchuk family tradition.

The bright humid late August day sharply clashed with the drab gray ugliness of Workmen's Circle cemetery.

Forty mourners crammed between the headstones and surrounded Morris Fish's coffin, which was suspended by a hydraulic device over the open grave. Charlie, Celia in her wheelchair, and Rabbi Schwarz were closest to the casket.

"Why did he die?" Celia cried out, creating a chain reaction of sympathetic sobs throughout the crowd.

"Why did he die? Why did he die?" she shouted.

To Charlie, his mother's cries were rehearsed, false.

He thought about the old kindergarten song, "There Was an Old Lady who Swallowed a Fly."

He didn't know why this song came to him.

"Why did he die? Why did he die?" she screamed. The crowds' sobs grew in intensity.

I don't know why he swallowed a fly, perhaps he'll die.

Charlie smiled at the goofy song playing in his head.

Hands pushed past him, stroking and patting Celia's frail back and shoulders, shoving Charlie away from her.

"Why did he die?" she wailed.

"He swallowed a spider to catch the fly. It wiggled and jiggled and giggled inside him. Perhaps he'll die."

A giggle escaped from Charlie's lips.

His Aunt Beatrice glared at him.

He wanted to smash his aunt's face. He wanted to kick over his mother's wheelchair.

The Rabbi began Kaddish, the prayer for the dead. Several other male voices chimed in. Charlie tried to follow along as best as he could. To get through his bar mitzvah, he had learned Hebrew phonetically.

Celia looked up and scanned the mourners to see who was saying Kaddish. Her eyes locked on Ted Fish, Morris's older brother.

Her face changed from grief to rage. She pointed at him. Her finger trembled. "No! You don't deserve to pray for him, you rat! Where the hell were you when he needed you?"

Ted Fish recoiled as if slapped. He tried to speak. Only a few words squeaked out of his throat. "I'm sorry."

Ted Fish looked almost exactly like Morris but much taller—almost a foot taller.

"Get out of here, you rat!" Celia yelped.

Ted Fish reeled back, almost stumbling over a headstone.

"Mrs. Fish, please," the rabbi begged in a loud whisper.

Celia pulled her body up from the wheelchair. She shook a frail fist at Ted Fish. "Go to hell!"

"No, mother! Don't!" This was the first real emotion that Charlie had felt from his mother on this day.

He pushed through the mourners and threw his arms

around her. Her body was stiff with cold anger, unresponsive to his hug.

"No, he's not worth it. Dad wouldn't want it this way."

She pushed him away. "What do you know about your father? You know nothing about him! You know nothing about his lousy family! How they humiliated me!"

• 1966 •

GRANDMA RIFKA FISH'S casket was inside the lead hearse parked in front of Machpelach Cemetery's memorial chapel. A second hearse for immediate family members was parked behind it. The rear passenger doors were wide open.

Mourners exited the one-story nondescript chapel building. Beatrice Sternbaum and her husband Sheldon, and Ted Fish and his wife Esther were at the head of the pack. They entered the hearse, closing the doors behind them.

Charlie, his mother, and his father were among the last mourners to straggle out of the chapel. Charlie pushed his mother's wheelchair.

Celia was crying too hard for the occasion; she really never liked Grandma Rifka. Behind Celia's back, Grandma Rifka used to call her "the cripple."

Morris Fish was visibly moved. His eyes were red-rimmed. His nose was running. His cocky John Garfield tough guy strut was gone. He moved cautiously, his body heaving with each step.

Charlie had never seen his father so emotionally devastated, even at Grandpa Aaron's funeral five years earlier.

Through her "grief," Celia Fish noticed Morris's brother and sister sitting inside the second hearse. "There's Beatrice and Ted," she said to Morris, then waved to the relatives.

The Sternbaums and Fishes didn't wave back. Beatrice Sternbaum turned her head away. Ted Fish's face flushed a deep shade of red.

Celia always felt socially inferior to the Fishes, especially to Beatrice Sternbaum. Her sister-in-law was a Wayne State University graduate. Celia had dropped out of high school in eleventh grade, after her mother died.

"We'll ride with Bea and Sheldon," said Celia to Charlie and her husband. Charlie pushed her wheelchair toward the hearse. Morris followed, his gaze downcast.

Ted Fish's eyes frantically searched the crowd of mourners as his brother approached the hearse.

"Hesh! Heshy!" Ted bellowed and waved.

Herschel Gelbfiscz, a distant cousin who worked as an assistant manager at Ted's East Detroit supermarket, walked to the hearse.

He was a roly-poly man who had never lost his old country accent. His tiny dour wife, Belle, was with him.

"C'mon, Heshy! Belle! Get inside!" shouted Ted Fish.

"'You sure dot dere's room, Ted?" shrugged Herschel Gelbfiscz.

"Yeah. Yeah. There's plenty of room!" Ted opened the passenger door for them. The Gelbfisczs climbed inside.

"What are *they* doing in that hearse?" Celia whimpered to Charlie.

Morris Fish jerked to a stop, as if blindsided. Charlie stopped, too.

"C'mon, Morris, Charles. It's a big car. There's still room inside," Celia insisted. Charlie moved the wheelchair toward the hearse.

"Wait for us, Ted!" Celia called out with a bright smile.

"Hurry, Morris. You don't want them to leave without us," she called over her shoulder.

Morris Fish followed tentatively.

Ted Fish smiled at Celia, but looked straight at his brother. "Sorry. No room."

All color drained from Celia's face. "Bea?" she pleaded for an opinion from her sister-in-law.

Beatrice Sternbaum looked away.

Ted Fish reached over laps and slammed the passenger door shut.

The lead hearse's engine started with a roar. The family hearse started with a louder roar.

"Of all the nerve!" whined Celia.

Morris Fish began to sob.

Charlie had never seen his father cry out loud. He walked to his father and put his arm around his shoulders. "The hell with 'em, dad. They're cockroaches," he said quietly.

Morris sobbed harder, his shoulders shaking violently. Charlie hugged him tight. "You don't need them. You've got me and mom."

"Charles! Morris! Let's go to our car! The funeral procession is starting!" said Celia.

Charlie gave his father one last squeeze, then released him. "Let's go, dad. Let's show 'em that we're bigger than the whole bunch put together. They can all go to hell!" Charlie said this in a clear enunciated tone for all in earshot.

"Watch your mouth, young man. We're in public," said Celia through clenched teeth.

Morris's tentative steps accelerated to his normal stride. Charlie pushed the wheelchair. They headed for his father's brand new Pontiac Bonneville in the chapel parking lot.

On this day of his grandmother's funeral, Charlie eased into his "legacy" of being the black sheep son of the black sheep.

• 1976 •

AFTER THE RABBI and all the mourners had drifted away, Charlie and his mother lingered by his father's casket, which was still suspended over the open grave. Celia was quiet, all cried out. Charlie stared at a solitary cloud in the bright blue summer sky, a meditation focus exercise that he picked up during a brief 1969 encounter with Transcendental Meditation. He felt weak.

A cemetery groundskeeper in a filthy uniform ambled over. He was an obese man with a yarmulke worn lopsided on the back of his huge skull. His face was a bored placid mask, a wad of tobacco crammed inside his cheek.

He walked to the casket. Celia looked up with an expression of horror. "Wait!"

Charlie's "meditation" ended with a jolt, as the groundskeeper flicked a switch on the hydraulic device. Morris Fish's casket slowly lowered into the grave with a metallic drone.

"Stop!" Celia sobbed. "I need more time."

The groundskeeper stared dully at her. A small smile formed on his slack lips. He shrugged his fat shoulders. "Jus' doin' my job," he mumbled.

Anguish filled Charlie. He tried to move toward the worker, but his feet felt too heavy.

The fat man hawked out a stream of tobacco juice that landed on the mound of earth next to the grave. He smirked and walked away.

"Hey, you!" a male voice shouted from a short distance behind Charlie and his mother. A wiry dark handsome man in a navy blue conservative suit moved through the maze of headstones like a football quarterback. The man bolted after the groundskeeper, overtaking the much larger man.

Charlie and Celia could see that the men were engaged in a sharp exchange of words.

The maintenance worker pushed the smaller man in the chest. The wiry dark man nabbed the front of the fat man's filthy shirt, and delivered a sharp forehead-butt into the center of his face. The groundskeeper's eyes blinked in shock as a stream of blood ran from each nostril.

He moved toward his much smaller attacker, then hesitated. There was a stare-down between the two men. The malevolent look on the big man's face changed to fear. The smaller man's dark murderous gaze bore two laser holes deep into the man's eyes. He retreated.

The stranger turned to Charlie and Celia. He placed a hand over his heart, nodded at them, and left.

"Who was that?" Celia asked quietly.

"I've never seen him before," said Charlie.

There was something familiar about the stranger. The eyes. Was he one of the Chicago relatives that he had seen only briefly at a family party? The stranger looked more Sicilian than Jewish. Although he was five or six years younger than Charlie, he might have been one of his father's gambling buddies. Throughout the years, Morris Fish had always found "surrogate sons" for discussions of baseball scores, league standings, and batting averages.

Charlie always felt that he had left a void in his father's life. He wasn't the son whom Morris Fish dreamed of.

•:•

after the funeral

· 1976 ·

AFTER THE BURIAL, friends and family members gathered at Celia Fish's Oak Park apartment.

Celia referred to this small drab two-bedroom apartment as a "townhouse." It was one of two hundred units in a drab brown brick complex, located only two blocks from the Westridge Street house where Charlie grew up. The "townhouse" was a steep step down the economic ladder for the Fishes. Celia told her friends that "it made no sense to maintain a house" after Charlie left for Eastern Michigan University. The reality was that Morris Fish had lost most of their savings.

The "townhouse" was crammed with people. Card tables, folding chairs, and the trays of food from Sol's Restaurant had appeared almost magically in the apartment living room, courtesy of Charlie's Aunt Beatrice. Family members, friends, and neighbors loaded up their plates with bagels slathered with cream cheese and smoked fish.

Aunt Beatrice had assumed full authority over all the post-funeral activities, shouting orders like a Marine drill instructor to Charlie and all other relatives under forty years old.

At the rear of the living room, Celia reclined on her coveted lime green couch. The couch's plastic covering had yellowed over the years.

Wellwishers, sympathizers, and near-strangers lined up to pay their respects to her. Celia had prepared a highly detailed story about her husband's death. "He was sitting right here on this couch. Charles was home for dinner and he was kibbitzing around with Morris, like he always does . . . we thought he was laughing. Morris was always laughing at Charles' *narishkeit*. But he wasn't laughing. He was gasping for air. Charles tried mouth-to-mouth, but it was no use. I called the paramedics, but it was too late. He died right where I'm sitting . . . at the emergency room, they said that his aorta had ruptured. If you remember, he had that terrible open heart surgery in Cleveland . . ."

She repeated this lie to anyone who would listen.

Charlie wanted to shout out the truth, but he had promised his mother that the real nature of his father's death would be one of many "family secrets."

"We're running out of salmon! Go to Sol's! Right now!" Aunt Beatrice's foghorn voice bellowed, as she stuffed a crisp one-hundred-dollar bill into Charlie's suit jacket pocket.

Celia's neighbors, Mrs. Freitag and Mrs. Leibowitz, traded gossip and innuendoes in too-loud whispery voices. Charlie couldn't help staring at Mrs. Freitag's tongue. The cream cheese had turned it white.

Cousin Herschel Gelbfiscz repeated one phrase over and over to anyone that would listen. "Da lest time I seen

Morris he vas healthy like Black Engus bool, a *shtarker* all his life."

Charlie was horrified. These strangers, these moochers, these foul-weather friends surrounded him. The last thing that he wanted to do was play host to them. A bagels-and-fish run to Sol's was the excuse that he needed to escape all the meaningless chatter.

He climbed into his new Datsun B-210, known fondly as "the Bumblebee." It was a sturdy yet dinky banana yellow vehicle, Japan's answer to the VW Beetle.

Owning a Japanese car in the middle of an auto industry recession was a sacrilege in the Detroit metropolitan area. A variety of foot-sized dents marred the Datsun's body.

He had bought the car a month earlier with the meager earnings from his job in the city of Detroit's urban planning department. Charlie painted cartoon murals on the walls of decaying storefronts in rundown Detroit commercial districts — an ironic turn of events since the old days of desecrating the one-room schoolhouse and other Oak Park buildings with Joe Murphy.

The Bumblebee rattled along Ten Mile Road toward the newly opened "Southfield branch" of Sol's Restaurant.

Charlie turned up the volume on his car radio. WRIF was playing Jimi Hendrix's "Electric Ladyland." This was a rarity. What used to be "underground Detroit radio" had been transformed into cheery d.j. yack and a slick commercial power-rock playlist. The likes of Journey, America, Starship, and Wings had replaced the Beatles, Jefferson Airplane, Janis, The Mothers of Invention, and even Led Zeppelin.

The hippies had come and gone. Charlie felt as if he'd become a thirty-year-old anachronism. He hated the Seventies. Everybody in the suburbs was smoking dope and flashing the peace sign: lawyers, doctors, housewives, rednecks, Republicans. The counterculture had become chic.

Charlie's Datsun passed the "Southfield City Limits" sign. The sight of the encroaching suburban landscape sickened him.

He parked the Bumblebee in front of Sol's Restaurant at the newly constructed Buckingham Palace strip mall on Lahser. The Southfield Sol's was half the size of the old Oak Park restaurant.

Sol Shribman had sold the original place in 1969 when the neighborhood began to "change." Blacks, working-class orthodox Jews, new Russian immigrants, and Chaldeans had moved in. Arabic script replaced Hebrew script on many of the store signs along Nine Mile Road. The original Sol's had become a rib joint. The banquet hall had become an industrial laundry plant. Although he hated Oak Park, Charlie hated witnessing its deterioration more.

Sol Shribman had opened a separate and larger banquet facility, the Canterbury House, on Woodward Avenue in tony Birmingham. The new banquet hall was built in an "Olde English" style and catered to as many fancy gentile parties as fancy Jewish parties.

Charlie entered the Southfield Sol's Restaurant. Two trays laden with lox, cream cheese, and smoked fish were waiting for him at the deli counter.

∵

H E arrived at his mother's apartment with the deli trays. In the living room, Lowell Krantz was sitting on the couch, his arm draped affectionately over Celia's shoulders.

Charlie almost dropped the trays. He hated everything about Lowell Krantz.

Unlike the other males in the apartment, Krantz wasn't wearing a dark suit. He was wearing burgundy tennis shorts and a matching designer cabana shirt-jac. He came fresh from one of his daily tennis matches at the Greenmeadows Country Club in Bloomfield Hills. Beads of tennis sweat were still on his forehead.

Fifty-five-year-old Lowell Krantz was in top physical shape, handsome in an artificial way: a year-round tan, a perfectly fitted Hollywood-style pompadour hairpiece, and beautiful white capped teeth.

"Hey, Butchie!" Krantz bellowed.

Butchie was an annoying nickname from Charlie's early childhood.

"Hello, Mr. Krantz," Charlie mumbled as he set the trays down on a card table.

"What's with the 'Mr. Krantz'? C'mere! I wanna talk to you!"

Charlie walked reluctantly over to the couch.

Krantz pecked Celia's cheek. "This is my best gal pal, Butchie. Did you know that?"

Celia smiled weakly, eating up his cheap flattery as she always did.

Krantz stood up and bear-hugged Charlie, slapping him heartily on the back. "Listen, kid, I'm sorry about your old man. He was a good guy. My old buddy-buddy."

Charlie pulled back from him. "Yeah, he was your old buddy-buddy," He repeated Krantz's words without inflection.

"Hey, Butch, let's talk in the other room you an' me." He put his arm around Charlie's shoulders and steered him into Celia's bedroom.

Krantz shut the door behind them. "So, how are you and your mom fixed, kid? You need anything?"

"No. Not really, Mr. Krantz."

"Lowell! For godsakes, call me Lowell! I known you all your life! We're family! Your father an' I grew up together on Hastings Street! Your grandparents were like second parents to me! Morris was my brother!" He reached into his cabana shirt-jac pocket and retrieved a fat gambler's roll of hundred-dollar bills. He removed the platinum money clip and extended the roll to Charlie. "This is for your mother."

"No!" Charlie pushed the wad away.

"Are you *meshuga*? . . . Listen to me, Butch. Take it!"

Charlie's gut burned. "I can't accept this."

Lowell Krantz's jaw muscles clenched in anger. "Why not? Your father woulda done the same for my kids, if the shoe was on the other foot."

"I won't take your charity."

Krantz's year-round tan turned deep purple. His face quivered with rage. "Charity? I loved your father more than my own family!"

"Then why did you take all his money?"

"What? What the hell does that mean? I never took nothin' from your father. He always played even-Steven with me."

"That's not what the guys at the Produce Club told me."

"What 'guys'?"

"Tony Scotto, Billy Clark, to name a few."

"Jesus Christ! You mean you're gonna believe a bunch of drunk *goyim* at the Produce Club over me, who's known you all your life?"

"Yes."

"Why you snot-nosed . . . " Lowell Krantz spit out the words, then stopped short. He exhaled and regained his composure. "Listen, kid, I know you're upset. That's why you're saying this malarkey. Take the goddamn money!"

He threw the wad at Charlie. Hundred-dollar bills scattered all over Celia's bed.

Krantz stormed out of the bedroom, slamming the door behind him.

Charlie stared at the hundred-dollar bills. There had to be at least two thousand dollars on the bed.

He could remember all the hundred-dollar bills in his father's Produce Club poker pots.

•••

• 1963 •

ALTHOUGH MORRIS FISH was neither a produce worker
nor a butcher, he was an almost-daily "guest" at the Produce
Club.

In the Thirties, Forties, and most of the Fifties, the
Produce Club was an illegal nightly poker game for produce workers and butchers held in three dingy rooms above
the Cattleman's Bar in Detroit's downtown Eastern Market
terminal. Each of the three card rooms were filled with card
tables and whiskey-drinking tough guys betting serious
money. Food and booze were amply supplied by the
Cattleman's Bar downstairs.

In 1959, the Produce Club moved to larger quarters on
Eight Mile Road, closer to the northwest suburbs. The new
facility was once a health club called the Mercury Spa,
which mostly consisted of two Olympic-sized swimming
pools, one indoors and one outdoors, providing year-round
swimming "open to the public."

On hot summer days, Charlie Fish would borrow Joe
Murphy's St. Christopher medal and ride his bike to the
Mercury Spa swimming pool. He'd sign in as "Charlie
Rossi." The owners of the Mercury Spa didn't like Jews. A
sign over the check-in desk said "Gentiles Only."

After the Produce Club bought the Mercury Spa, they
did a full renovation, adding a steam room, a dry heat
sauna, a barbershop, a large plush card room, and a mem-
bers-only Italian restaurant. The Club owners brought the

chef in from Lelli's Restaurant on Woodward. Charlie loved the veal Parmesan.

The Club's membership expanded beyond the Eastern Market crowd and it became a hangout for all who could afford the hefty monthly dues, including politicians, professional athletes, dentists, mob guys, and full-time gamblers like Morris Fish. There were even a couple of black members, a doctor and a lawyer.

Only women couldn't become members. Spouses and daughters of members were only allowed in the Italian restaurant and the pool area.

The buxom young girls who brought drinks and burgers to the cardplayers were the exception. They were allowed in forbidden parts of the Club. Occasionally hookers would show up for special occasions, but this was kept under wraps.

Charlie enjoyed going to the Produce Club. He especially enjoyed wearing a Star Of David on a chain when he swam in the former Mercury Spa pools.

He also enjoyed sitting in the *shvitz*, or steam room, listening to the old *kockers* swap lies and tell dirty jokes.

Occasionally, Charlie would sneak a peek into the card room. Morris wouldn't allow him inside. Poker was serious business for his father. He didn't like to be disturbed.

Players at a typical Morris Fish poker game might include Sal Ventimiglia, reputed head of Detroit's Black Hand; Judge Nathan Greenburg, "best friend of the Detroit Police Department" and the Black Hand; Swabby Slim, the host of the local Popeye the Sailor TV cartoon show; and

Lawrence J. Horton, former State of Michigan treasurer, with his two artificial legs laid across a chair next to him.

Lowell Krantz would briefly sit in on all of the games in the Produce Club's card room; but he really didn't care for gambling. Krantz was "the house," one of the Club's "silent owners." He gambled only enough to be "one of the boys." His real function in the card room was to provide convenient high-interest loans to busted-out card players. Lowell Krantz was a loan shark. This was the root of his wealth.

The last time Charlie visited the Produce Club was also the first time that he'd ever seen his father physically scared.

On the day before the Fourth of July, Charlie spent the entire afternoon either dog paddling in the Club's outdoor pool or sitting in a beach chair reading Mad Magazine and drinking cherry cokes.

"Hey, Charlie!" Morris Fish's head poked out of the door to the indoor pool. His hair was wet.

The indoor pool was closed and locked up during the summer months.

"C'mon, kid. We gotta go!" said Morris. Charlie sensed the urgency in his father's voice, scrambled out of his chair, and entered the indoor pool area. Morris Fish was fully clothed in his favorite sharkskin suit, and soaking wet from the waist up.

Charlie was terrified by his father's frantic and frazzled appearance. "Dad? Why are you wet like that?"

"Shut up. We gotta get outta here." His father's voice was a harsh whisper. He gestured with his head, jerking his chin upward.

Charlie looked up and saw Lowell Krantz and two huge mean-faced black men standing in an observation window above the indoor pool area. Krantz's usual buddy-buddy smile was gone. His arms were folded angrily over his chest.

"Quick!" Morris grabbed Charlie's arm and dragged him through the pool area, through the Club's towel room and laundry service, and out a back door to an alley.

"Run!" Morris screamed at him.

Father and son ran to the parking lot and scrambled inside Morris's Pontiac Bonneville.

Morris frantically started the car. The engine roared as he gunned it. The Pontiac screeched out of the lot, cutting off several cars on Eight Mile Road.

Charlie saw the panic in his father's eyes. He knew that Krantz's two "friends" had just given his father an impromptu "swimming lesson." He knew that this beef was about money, gambling money.

• 1976 •

ON THE LAST day of his life, Morris Fish had played poker at the Produce Club.

Several of his father's poker buddies had come on this second day of shiva to Celia's apartment to pay their respects. Charlie liked some; others he liked only a little more than he liked Lowell Krantz. He sat on the living room couch and allowed them to gladhand him.

The doorbell rang.

Ringing a doorbell at a house of shiva wasn't done. Front doors were never locked. Usually gentiles made this mistake. It was probably more of Morris Fish's pals from the Produce Club.

Charlie went to the door, and was pleasantly surprised to see his old friend Joe Murphy. "Hey, Gefilte Fish."

They hugged.

"Sorry about the old man, Charlie. He was a cool guy, one of the original rebels."

Joe strode into the apartment living room. Everyone stopped chattering and stared at him.

Joe Murphy was a dramatic sight, with arms as large as horse legs and a luxuriant waist-length mane of dyed platinum-blonde Gorgeous George hair. For ten years he had made his living as a professional wrestler named "Killer Carver." For a couple of years he was even the champ of his midwestern wrestling circuit.

Celia looked up, her eyebrows knitted together. Annoyance penetrated through her grief. After all these years, she still hated Joe Murphy.

"I gotta get outta here," Charlie whispered to him.

"We'll take a ride, man," said Joe. "But, first I gotta say a few words to your mom."

Joe walked to the couch. Celia's eyes widened in horror. His eccentric childhood behavior had blossomed into full-blown Big Time Wrestling weirdness.

Joe Murphy kneeled down on one knee in front of Celia, took her hand, and kissed it; a gallant gesture that should've flattered her but didn't. Her face twisted into an expression of disgust.

"Thank you for stopping by," she said coldly, stiffly.

"I'll be back in a little while, mother. I'm going with Joe," said Charlie.

Celia's chin quivered. "Don't leave, Charles. I need you," she whimpered.

"I need a break." he headed to the door. "Sorry."

Aunt Beatrice blocked Charlie's path, a malevolent look on her face. She was several inches taller and several pounds heavier than him. "You're not going anywhere, Charles. Stay with your mother," she said this under her breath.

"My mother is surrounded by people who love her. She can carry on without me for an hour."

"Don't you dare leave," she growled.

"Aunt Beatrice, I gotta take care of myself."

"Why, you selfish . . ." she spat out these words.

"Damn right, I'm selfish. It's about time I took care of myself. Everybody forgot about me. He was my father. You and everyone else are treating me like an errand boy."

"It's about time that you learned how to be responsible. I know all about you and your drugs!"

"Yes, and I plan on getting good and high. Why do I have to be the Man of Steel? Can't I feel like crap too? *He was my goddamn father!*" He said these last words at full volume, bringing all conversation to a halt.

Aunt Beatrice recoiled at the violence of his words.

Charlie brushed her aside and left the apartment.

Joe Murphy smiled a goofy grin at everyone in the living room, shrugged his shoulders apologetically, and followed Charlie out the door.

••

JOE'S battered VW microbus traveled at a breakneck speed down the long stretch of unpaved Novi rural road. Charlie was always amazed at how close "the sticks" were to Detroit. The van's mufflerless engine rasped like a gravel grinder.

The interior of the microbus was an impenetrable fog of dope smoke. The sounds of Elmore James's "The Sky Is Crying" blasted out of Joe's eight-track player.

Joe shouted above the music. "Darla wanted to come by and pay her respects, but you know her. Can't handle even minor cosmic interference, man."

"Yeah, what else is new?" Charlie sighed.

"She still loves you, Charlie."

"I love her too, but I guess I'm just more cosmic interference to her . . . is the latest shrink helping at all?" Charlie turned down the volume of the tape player.

"She's been through two shrinks since the last time you saw her. We had to move her into the house, otherwise she'd be on the street again. It was Lucy's idea. I married a good woman. I don't know how she can put up with it. Darla drives me fucking nuts. The crazy gene runs wild through the female side of my family. No cure, pal." Joe passed a cigar-sized joint to Charlie.

"Like you're sane, right, Joe?" he smiled.

I wouldn't be friends with you, Gefilte Fish, if I was sane, man."

"Maybe Darla is the sane one. Did you ever think of that? The State of Michigan gives her disability money every month, right? No cares. No responsibilities. Fuck the world." He took a deep drag on the Jamaican joint.

"That's a different way of looking at a load of bullshit." Joe spit out the van window.

Charlie passed the joint back to Joe and changed the subject. "So, are you still winning all your matches, Frankenstein?"

"The day after I turned thirty, the fucking pencil-neck promoters made me become a villain. Why do you think I got this fruitcake hair?"

Charlie laughed. "You make a good villain, man."

"Crap. I'm getting too old for this physical shit. All these young guys coming in are twice my size. These meatballs don't know dick about real wrestling moves. It's all brute force superhero crap. They're all mouth."

"My dad and I used to watch Big Time Wrestling every Saturday afternoon.."

"Remember The Sheik, man? Dick the Bruiser? Jumpin' Johnny Jones? Those guys had style. Jumpin' Johnny taught me everything. He was a fucking physical comedy genius like Chaplin. A master acrobat. Learned all his shit from all those great Mexico City wrestlers. Little guys that moved with expertise. You know what Johnny's doing now? He's in a goddamn trailer in Port Huron whacked out on painkillers.

Can you believe it? Fucker broke every bone in his body at one time or another, but did the pencil-neck bastard promoters give him a pension or insurance? Hell no."

"You're in a tough business, man."

"And those pin-dick fans they think it's all fixed and we walk away from this shit with our balls intact. Sure, we know who's gonna win and who's gonna lose, but we take our bumps just like goddamn prizefighters. Did you know that I broke my neck five years ago when I was working down in the Deep South circuit?"

"I didn't know that," Charlie gasped.

"It's a miracle that I healed, but I learned something, that I ain't gonna wind up like Jumpin' Johnny. I'm trying to convince them goddamn pencil-necks in the front office to make me an announcer. The fans think I'm funny. I'd be a natural announcer."

"For what its worth, you always make me laugh, Frankenstein."

"You woulda made a good wrestler too, Gefilte Fish, if you weren't such a goddamn shrimp."

"Yeah. Sure," Charlie laughed.

"Remember that fuckin' 'Donald Duck'?"

"Who the hell could forget?" said Charlie.

∵

1961

Joe Murphy

• 1961 •

JUNIOR HIGH GYM class was torture for Charlie Fish and
Joe Murphy. The teacher, Mr. Slezak, was a former
Marine Corps drill instructor and ran his class with the
same discipline.

Coach Slezak was a scary guy. His body was a squat taut
coil of muscles. His face resembled a flat slab of unpolished
red granite. His eyes were deep-set angry shadows. His teeth
were yellow nicotine-stained stubs. His breath smelled of
black coffee and Chesterfield cigarettes. His voice was a
lisping rasp, spittle flying randomly whenever he was agitat-
ed, which was often. His students called him "Donald
Duck" behind his back.

Charlie Fish and Joe Murphy hated Coach Slezak.
Above all, they hated the shrill tin whistle that he wore on
a leather cord around his neck.

While Charlie's flat feet and lack of enthusiasm made
him unable to excel in even the least strenuous sports, Joe
Murphy was athletic, but hated anything smacking of
authority and team spirit.

He joined Charlie at Oak Park High after being kicked
out of Our Lady Of Mercy Catholic School for an unusually filthy sketch of Sister Regina engaged in one of the
more double-jointed positions of the Kama Sutra.

Korkis and Rothman, Charlie's enemies, were also in
Slezak's gym class.

One Friday morning, Slezak announced that students

would participate in a series of "Greco-Roman-thtyle colle-giate wrethling matcheth, that will take place nextht Monday morning."

"Gentlemen, I have paired up boyth according to weight and height. Each match will latht two minutes, or until one boy'th shoulderth are pinned to the mat for a ten count. In the event that there ith no pin-down, I will determine the winner of the match."

Charlie hated Slezak even more after the Coach paired him with David Rothman. He knew how much Charlie feared physical violence and David Rothman.

Joe Murphy was matched with Psycho Bobby Shapiro, the only seventh grader with a US Navy tattoo and a five o'clock shadow.

Charlie had two days to ponder his fate. He thought about taking his newspaper route money and boarding a bus for New York City, the home of Mad, DC Comics, and Famous Monsters of Filmland. He thought about dropping his father's Brunswick bowling ball on his left foot to earn a doctor's letter that would get him out of Slezak's class for the rest of the year. He thought about going to the bathroom medicine cabinet, and swallowing all of his mother's pills.

•••

ON Monday morning, Charlie showed up for gym class.

In the locker room, David Rothman took bets, not on *if* he'd win the match, but how quickly. Rothman bet that he'd pin Charlie in twenty seconds or less.

Joe Murphy and "Howieschultz," the tiny orthodox Jewish kid that was Korkis and Rothman's other main torment-target, pooled a $30 bet. In high school, Howie Schultz wasn't called Howie or Schultzy. He was called "Howieschultz" — one word.

The betting and raucous laughter at his expense made Charlie physically ill. He ran to the lavatory, went into a stall, and tried to puke, but could only dry-heave.

∵

A square of foam-filled mats covered the center of the gym floor. The boys, clad in red shorts and T-shirts, squatted in a circle around the mats. David Rothman joked with his buddies and smiled sadistically at Charlie Fish.

A cold nervous sweat formed on Charlie's forehead. Joe Murphy whispered advice in his left ear, "Use the hard parts of your body — your elbows, your knees, your thick head. Go for his guts, his nuts, his throat. Donald Duck will never see it."

"Jesus," Charlie groaned.

"Kill him," Howieschultz urged into his right ear.

Charlie's match was the second one of the day. He watched in horror as eighty-pound Skinny Sam Deutsch, star of the Oak Park High debate team, got tied into a human sailor's knot by 110-pound Barry Berger, the Oak Park High baseball team's star shortstop. Skinny Sam screamed for mercy. Slezak blew his whistle and the match ended in less than sixty seconds. Skinny Sam fought back his tears of humiliation. Barry

Berger jumped up and down, savoring his quick brutal victory. The hoods guffawed. Slezak blasted his whistle to quiet the boys. Skinny Sam hobbled to a remote corner of the gym and sat in a dejected heap

Korkis and Rothman stared straight at Charlie. Rothman smirked and smacked his right fist into his left palm.

"Okay, Rothman an' Fish, it'th your turn!" said Slezak.

Charlie reluctantly pulled himself to his feet. Joe Murphy slapped him on the back. "Go get him, Gefilte Fish. He ain't nothin' but a goddamn pussy."

Rothman trotted onto the mat, his fingers flashing "V"s for victory. Korkis and the other hoods cheered.

Slezak flipped a coin and Charlie called "tails." It came up "heads." Rothman was given the more advantageous on-top starting position in the classic Greco-Roman wrestling style. Charlie dropped to his hands and knees in a horsie stance. Rothman winked at his friends and dropped to one knee next to Charlie. He wrapped his arm around Charlie's waist and squeezed his stomach. Charlie grunted. His face turned red. He hated that Rothman was touching him. He hated the submissive position that he was in.

"Roll over on your back an' let me pin you quick, Fish, if you know what's good for you," Rothman rasped into his ear.

"Are you boyth ready?" asked Slezak.

Charlie and Rothman nodded.

Slezak blasted his whistle and the match began.

Rothman used the body leverage of the top position to smash Charlie's face straight into the mat. Rothman plunked his ass onto Charlie's back. With a shout of rage, Charlie placed his palms on the mat and did a push-up, throwing Rothman off him. As he tried to scramble to his feet, Rothman charged at him. He rammed his head right into Charlie's balls, driving him ass-first back onto the mat. Charlie screamed in pain and anger. As Rothman scrambled onto his body for a quick pin, Charlie grabbed him by both shoulders and flipped him onto his back. He was surprised at how light his enemy was, and how weak his resistance. He straddled Rothman's chest and plopped both knees onto his shoulders, pinning him solidly to the mat. Rothman struggled, but couldn't break free. Slezak beat the mat ten times with the flat of his beefy hand, then blew his whistle.

Charlie rolled off David Rothman. He had pinned him in less than one minute. Joe Murphy, Howieschultz, and several of Rothman's other victims cheered loudly. The hoods were silent.

David Rothman lay in motionless shock on the mat. Kids surrounded Charlie, slapping him on the back.

Slezak blew his whistle. The boys sat back down on the gym floor. Charlie beamed. He knew that his life in high school had changed.

He watched the other matches. Joe Murphy won a hard-fought match, pinning Psycho Bobby Shapiro barely within the two-minute time limit

After school, instead of beating each other's brains out, Joe and Psycho Bobby split a bottle of malt liquor in Oak Park Park.

When Charlie came home from school, he went straight to his bedroom, flopped down on his mattress, and fell into a deep sleep of victorious relief. Thinking that he was ill, his parents didn't wake him up.

The next day, he told his father about his victory on the wrestling mat. Morris knew that Charlie had been David Rothman's goat for years. Charlie remembered the day that he was walking with his father to the Eagle Dairy and he stepped off the sidewalk to let Rothman and Korkis pass. Charlie had never been more humiliated, and his father was never more ashamed of him.

To celebrate Charlie's wrestling victory, Morris took him to the Eagle Dairy in a near expression of poetic justice. They wolfed down the Eagle Dairy's specialty Bet-You-Can't-Eat-it-All Banana Split.

Charlie could never remember seeing his father so proud of him.

⋰

A couple of months later, Joe Murphy joined the school wrestling team. Charlie didn't. He didn't like violence, even if he was good at it.

• 1976 •

AT ONE A.M., after countless shots of Jack Daniels and joints of Jamaican, Joe Murphy dropped Charlie off at his mother's apartment.

The living room was empty and dark. The folding tables

were still in the center of the room, but there were no longer deli trays on them. Aunt Beatrice and Delphine, Celia's longtime black maid/nurse, did an excellent job cleaning up all traces of the day's shiva visitors.

Charlie felt bad that he had left his mother's "house of shiva." He tiptoed to her bedroom. He opened the door and peeked inside. Celia was sound asleep, a tiny fetus-shaped lump. Sadness washed over him. She looked so lonely in the king-sized bed that she had shared so long with her husband.

He felt bad for all the hatred that he had shown toward her throughout the years. He had mixed feelings toward her. He hated her for her pettiness, her stubbornness, her shallowness, her pretentiousness, her meanness. He loved her because she was his mother.

Charlie could hear the telephone ringing from the living room. Celia didn't stir.

The phone kept ringing.

Who could be calling at one A.M.? thought Charlie.

He went to the phone, and answered on the tenth ring. "Hello?"

There was only the sound of breathing on the other end of the line.

"Who is this?"

The breathing turned into an ominous quiet laugh. A stab of fear hit Charlie. He hung up the phone.

He could feel his heart pounding rapidly in his chest.

Charlie wondered, after all these years, if "the insanity" was beginning again. Or, were some mean kids making a random prank call?

He took the phone receiver off the hook and set it on the coffee table.

• 1957 •

THE PHONE CALLS began on the Monday before Charlie Fish's ninth birthday.

He came home from school.

His father was still at work. Delphine the maid had driven his mother to the Northland Shopping Center. Celia was probably at J.L. Hudson's buying Charlie's birthday presents, most likely an array of pastel colored sweaters that he'd wear only if forced.

He turned on the living room TV to watch one of his favorite shows, "The Cartoon Carnival." The host was "Willy Nilly," a failed stand-up comic whose real name was Eli Tukel. Despite the show's title, no cartoons were shown on The Cartoon Carnival, only two-reelers starring the Three Stooges, Laurel and Hardy, and the Little Rascals, along with more obscure two-reel comedies starring Andy Clyde, Edgar "Slow Burn" Kennedy, Benny Rubin, and Clark and McCullough.

"Willy Nilly" knew all the stories about these old vaudeville comedians. Charlie was fascinated by the stories and by "Willy Nilly." Watching Eli Tukel's schizo act was like watching a man having a nervous breakdown. "Willy Nilly" would have "conversations" with his own tape-recorded characters: Crusher, Gumbo, and Herkimer.

"You're a stupid idiot, Willy Nilly!" Crusher taunted from an offstage tape recorder.

"Sticks and stones will break my bones, but names will always make me cry! Boo hoo hoo!" Willy Nilly fake-blubbered.

"*I'll* break your bones, you simp!" croaked Crusher.

The living room telephone interrupted The Cartoon Carnival.

Charlie ignored the ringing phone. It was probably another call from one of his mother's dippy gossipy tranquilizer-addled bored housewife friends.

The phone kept ringing.

Charlie cursed under his breath. He picked up the receiver. "Hello?"

There was only the sound of slowly inhaling and exhaling breath.

"Hello? Who's there?"

"I'm gonna kill you if your old man doesn't pay up," a voice whispered.

"Is this you, Frankenstein?" Charlie laughed.

"I'll kill you and your mother," a guttural edge was added to the whisper.

"This isn't funny, Joe."

"My name ain't Joe. I'll cut your goddamn throat open, you little bastard, you hear me? Tell your old man!" The whisper was louder and harsher. It wasn't Joe Murphy's voice.

Charlie slammed down the phone.

He figured that it was probably another one of Rothman and Korkis's mean pranks.

The phone rang again. He picked up the receiver on the second ring. "This isn't funny!" he shouted into it.

"You'll never see me coming, boy. I'll be in your bedroom when you're sleeping. I'll rip open your belly!" The voice laughed.

Charlie hung up. It wasn't Korkis or Rothman. He couldn't identify the voice as male or female, adult or kid, but he knew that the voice belonged to a maniac. A fearful sweat rolled down his forehead.

On the television, Edgar Kennedy's "slow burn" ignited. He was on a crazed rampage, throwing his shiftless brother-in-law through a picture window, tearing down all four walls of his living room with his bare hands.

The phone rang.

Charlie picked up the receiver, pressed down the cradle button, and left the phone off the hook.

∴

THE front door opened. Delphine pushed Celia's wheelchair inside. She was a football fullback-sized black woman with silver hair and a rollicking laugh that accompanied a savage sense of humor. Charlie loved Delphine. No matter how bad his day was, Delphine could make him laugh. Celia hated Delphine, but needed her. The woman was strong enough to stand up to Celia's stubborn behavior, and smart enough to handle Celia's many medical emergencies. In the Fish household, she wasn't a luxury, she was a necessity.

Delphine wheeled Celia into the living room.

Charlie was engrossed in a Shemp Three Stooge episode. He hated Shemp. Unlike Curly, there was nothing lovable about Shemp. Moe hammered a nail into Shemp's sickeningly ugly greasy head. Charlie could feel the skullbone-crunch sound effect.

"Charles, why is this phone off the hook?" Celia asked. She put the receiver back on the cradle.

"There were these crazy phone calls, Mommy."

"What crazy phone calls?"

Charlie picked up the phone receiver and set it on the coffee table.

"What are you doing? Don't you know that I was expecting an important call?" Celia put the receiver back on the cradle.

"He was threatening to kill us."

"Who?"

"I don't know, Mommy."

"My God. You're acting like a screwball again. I won't put up with it."

"Why won't you believe me, Mom? "

"I don't believe you because you're a liar. This is another one of your stories. Another way to get back at me. You hate me. You've always hated me."

The phone rang.

"Don't answer it!" Charlie shouted.

Celia picked up the phone.

Charlie gasped.

"Hello, Doris . . . yes, my phone was out of service for a few hours." She looked at Charlie and shook her head in disgust.

He ran to his bedroom and slammed the door behind him.

The maniac's phone calls stopped, at least for that day.

⋰

the second day
of shiva

· 1976 ·

AT 10:30 A.M., Celia Fish's apartment living room was packed with people.

Charlie shut and locked his mother's bedroom door for the sake of privacy. He was sitting on his parents' bed, examining a large manila envelope. The words "Personal Effects of Morris Fish" were printed in red magic marker on the envelope's face. A Detroit policeman had delivered it early that morning.

The Detroit police had only kept Morris's body for a twenty-four-hour observation period and determined, without an autopsy, that the gunshot was self-inflicted due to the nature of the powder burns and angle of trajectory. The jaded apathy of the Detroit police homicide squad was probably the largest part of their decision, thought Charlie. Morris Fish was just part of the daily body count.

He wanted to press the police for an autopsy. His mother didn't. He didn't want to prolong her grief, so he relented.

I don't need the goddamn cops, he thought. Fuck 'em. I don't need the autopsy either. I'll find out on my own.

He dumped the contents of the manila envelope onto

the bed: car keys, a black leather Las Vegas Desert Inn wallet, and a golf money clip with a pitiful roll of fourteen five-dollar bills. He knew that police, paramedics, or both probably ripped off Morris Fish in his last moments. His father had never carried less than five hundred dollars in his gambler's roll.

Charlie opened the black calfskin wallet and emptied its contents. Three quarters, a driver's license, and a plastic accordion of snapshots fell out. He probed the wallet with his index fingers for hidden compartments. There was a narrow pocket behind the wallet's change pouch. He slid his finger into the pocket and found a tiny folded square of paper.

He opened the paper to its full size. It was a photocopy of a typewritten I.O.U. dated six months before his father's death.

"I, Morris Jacob Fish, owe Lowell Sherwin Krantz the sum of $30,000."

His father's primitive signature scrawl was on the bottom of the page. Charlie stared at the paper. Morris Fish had never owned a typewriter and wouldn't have known how to use one if he did. He was a nearly illiterate sixth grade dropout.

Charlie wondered what kind of pressure his father was under when he signed the I.O.U. He knew that Morris Fish was flat broke at the time of his death. Charlie's failed year-and-a-half of law school provided him enough savvy to know that the terms of the "loan" weren't binding because the rate of interest, or consideration, wasn't included in the agreement; but Charlie knew that there was always a rate of interest when dealing with Lowell Krantz—an unreasonable rate of interest, or "vigorish" in the language of the underworld.

Did Krantz kill my father? he thought.

There was a loud knock on the bedroom door. "Charles, why is this door locked? There are guests out here! I need help," bellowed Aunt Beatrice's foghorn voice.

"In a minute," he grumbled.

He could hear his aunt's frustrated sigh. "Don't hibernate in there. Kaddish is about to start."

Charlie smoothed the wallet's plastic photograph "accordion" into a long flat strip. He examined the snapshots displayed in the strip's eight plastic sleeves.

In a 1945 wedding picture, Morris Fish looked trim and handsome in his Army uniform, despite recovering from a bout of Solomon Islands malaria. Celia looked radiant in her white traditional bridal gown and her natural raven black hair color, despite her bout with tuberculosis.

There was a wallet-sized version of Charlie's bar mitzvah portrait. A much larger oil painting version of it hung in a place of honor on his mother's apartment living room wall.

A yellowing pre-World War One photograph showed a thiry-five-year-old Grandpa Aaron posing proudly amidst the fully stocked shelves of canned goods in the American Flag Grocery Store, the East Detroit family business that he had started as an old-fashioned general store in 1901, and which eventually became a supermarket in 1951.

Morris Fish enlisted in the Army in 1940, leaving his father and brother Ted to run the family business. When he came back from the war, he wanted no part of the American Flag Grocery Store. The card room would be his place of business. He had honed his playing skills during "R and R" in gambling joints all over Sydney's King's Cross district. Charlie remembered his father's stories about Australia. Morris Fish had won a lot of poker money in Sydney. He came home with almost fifty thousand dollars in cash.

Charlie flipped over the plastic photo strip. There was only one photo on the other side of the strip: Morris Fish posing with a little boy on his lap, and the little boy wasn't Charlie.

He removed this photo from the plastic sleeve, and examined it closely. The baby's hair was black and thick like Charlie's, but as straight as an Indian's.

He turned over the photograph. A date was printed on the back: "June 10, 1956." He tucked the photo into his shirt pocket.

Another one of his father's secrets.

∵

· 1961 ·

AFTER A FEW years of quiet, the maniac's threatening phone calls started again.

Charlie and his parents were seated at the kitchen table for their traditional Friday night meal: pot roast and potatoes, Morris's favorite dish. Celia cooked all of the daily family meals. Despite her handicap, she moved nimbly in the kitchen.

The telephone rang. It was mounted on the kitchen wall at wheelchair-level for Celia's convenience. She answered.

"Hello," she twittered. The bright expression on her face turned to fear. "Who is this?" she said to the caller. Her fearful expression turned to horror.

She trembled and hung up the phone. "It's starting again, Morris."

Charlie's head began to pound. Months ago, almost immediately after the police and telephone company authorized a trace on the line, the calls had stopped. The police and phone company dismissed the calls as a random prank. Charlie wondered if the maniac had been tipped off about the trace.

The phone rang again. "Morris, answer it." Celia's voice quavered with horror. "You should've heard what that filthy pig said to me!"

"Take it off the hook." Morris shrugged his shoulders.

"No, I'm expecting an important call from Betty Bielfield."

The phone kept ringing. "Charlie's closer to the phone. Let him get it," grumbled Morris.

An icy terror filled Charlie. Since the last bout of maniac phone calls, he was still waking up in the middle of the night with screaming nightmares. The shrill telephone bell punctured his brain.

"Get the goddamn phone," Morris snapped at him.

"Okay. Okay." Charlie cursed under his breath and pushed his body off the wooden kitchen chair. He picked up the receiver and put it to his ear. "What do you want?" He tried to sound tough, but the tremble in his fourteen-year-old voice revealed his fear.

"Hello, Charlie," the voice oozed.

His head began to ache. The lunatic knew his name. This wasn't just a random prank as the police suggested.

"Whatsamatter with you, Charlie? Hang it up! Goddamn it!" shouted Morris.

"I don't understand." Celia said this more to herself. Her face was white with fear.

The maniac's voice spoke above a whisper for the first time, revealing its natural tone: either a mezzo female voice or a tenor male voice. "Would you like to talk to your brother, Charlie?"

"Brother? I don't have . . . " Charlie stopped in mid-sentence. He could hear the sound of a phone receiver being jostled, and the maniac talking to a third person off the line. Charlie listened closely.

"Say hello to your brother, Buddy . . . say hello." The

maniac's voice was a coo with no trace of meanness. Charlie identified this voice as female.

He could hear a young boy's voice in the background. "But I don't wanna talk, Mama."

"Goddamn it! I said, speak to your brother!" He could hear the harsh edge return to the maniac's voice.

Confused thoughts and emotions swirled inside Charlie's head. Do I have a brother? Is this baby my father's other son? My half-brother?

"Are you goddamn stupid, boy? I sez, hang up!" Morris snatched the phone from Charlie's hand and slammed it down onto the hook.

"Why is this happening?" sobbed Celia.

"And *you* shut up, woman! I'm tired of listening to your lousy whining!" he growled these words at her. The phone rang. Morris jerked the receiver from the hook and let it drop. It hit the linoleum kitchen floor, bounced up on its coiled cord, then was left to dangle. "It's stayin' off the hook. I don't give a good goddamn if Betty what's-her-name or any of them other phony balonies are supposed to call. You hear me, woman?"

A migraine squeezed Charlie's head. He ran to his bedroom and slammed the door behind him. He flung himself face down onto his bed. He tried to digest the mental and emotional chaos that surged through him. "She knows my name. This crazy bitch has to know my parents. What does she have against them? Why did she put that kid on the phone? Does my father have a separate family? Or is this the ravings of a sick bitch? Or maybe it's a nightmare created by one of my father's enemies?"

Charlie put the pillow over his face to muffle the confusion that he felt. Should I tell my mother what this lunatic bitch said to me? he asked himself. Should I tell her about the baby? Should I beat that goddamn cheating bastard's brains out!? Should I run away? Get the fuck out of this crazy house once and for all? Get the fuck out of Oak Park?

Morris Fish stomped into his son's bedroom, and locked the door behind him. "What the hell's going on with you, kid?"

Charlie clenched the pillow tighter over his face to drown out his father's voice.

Morris grabbed the pillow and pulled it off his son's face. He pushed his face close to Charlie's. "Talk to me, kid. What did she say to you?"

"Nothing." His voice broke. His father had called the maniac "she." He knew who the maniac was. Everything made more sense. Although Charlie had suspected it, for the first time he knew that his father was the one who had tipped her off about the police trace on the phone line.

Morris Fish's face was contorted with rage, and only an inch away from Charlie's face. "That's right, kid. As far as your mother is concerned, you heard nothing."

"Let me in! What's going on in there, Morris?" Celia's tiny fist beat weakly on the door.

"Just wait, Celia!" Morris shouted to her. Her knocking stopped.

Charlie's face turned an emotional shade of deep red. "Dad, do I have a brother?"

Morris squeezed his upper arms and pulled him to an upright position. Charlie winced in pain.

"Now listen to me, boy. I don't know what that woman said to you, but everything that comes out of her mouth is a damn lie. She's crazy in the head. *Meshuga*. I know her from the Club, but she's nuthin' to me. She's trash. A whore. She wants money from me. It's a con game. She's shakin' me down."

"She put a little kid on the line. Who is he?"

"She's got a buncha damn kids, all from different men. She don't even know who half the fathers are. She's crap. You gonna believe her over your own father?"

Charlie shook his head no.

"Listen to me, kid. When I get done with her she'll never bother your mother again. Take my word. I'll fix her once an' for all. So don't you say nothin' to your mother, you unnerstan?"

"Yes," he said this quietly, and rubbed his throbbing sinuses and wet eyes with his fists.

"So, do you believe me, kid?"

"Yes."

"'Yes what?" Morris shook him again.

"Yes, I believe you, Dad."

"That's better, kid." he smiled with relief, and kissed Charlie on the cheek. "I love you and your mother. You know that, right?"

"Yes, Dad."

"'You swear you're gonna keep this quiet?'"

"Yes."

"Okay, pal." Morris lifted himself off the bed. He unlocked and opened the bedroom door. Celia was sitting in her wheelchair, waiting in the hallway outside the bedroom. She was trembling like a wet puppy. Morris smiled at her and stroked her hair. "Don't worry, dear. I'll talk to the police tomorrow. Keep the phone off the hook just for tonight."

Celia nodded yes.

⁂

DESPITE his mother's protests, the phone number was changed to an unlisted one. The calls stopped, and Charlie felt some relief for a few weeks, until the day that "the visitors" began arriving.

Charlie came home from school. At 3:00 P.M. he had the house to himself. He turned on the TV. American Bandstand was on. He raised the volume to full blast. He liked filling every room in the house with rock and roll, even though he didn't like the mostly bland Bandstand teen idol "alternatives" to balls-out R&B; in this case, Bobby Rydell's "Venus in Blue Jeans." Charlie mostly watched American Bandstand for the Philly teenage dancing girls, especially Justine. She had mile-high blonde hair, slutty white lipstick, and exquisite pooched-out tits. Watching Justine's lips and tits gave him a boner, and, with his mother gone, he'd do something about it. He zipped down his fly and pulled out his pud. He approached the television set, penis in hand. He would squirt all over the TV screen, onto Justine's white lips.

The doorbell rang.

"Shit!" he groaned, as he pushed his stiff prick back into his pants.

The doorbell rang again.

Charlie walked to the door, opened it a crack, and peeked out. A sweaty middle-aged bald guy wearing an O Sole Mio Pizzeria shirt stood on the porch. He was holding a large pizza box. "O Sole Mio!" he called out.

Charlie opened the door wider. "Sorry, you have the wrong house."

The deliveryman's face turned sour. "This is 2303 Westridge, right?"

"We didn't order the pizza, mister." Charlie actually wished that he had three or four bucks to buy the pizza. He was getting hungry.

"Is this the Fish residence?" The man's eyebrows knitted together.

"Yes, but . . . "

"Then this is your pizza."

"I didn't order it. Maybe you got us confused. I have some cousins named Fish over on Scotia. Maybe they ordered the pizza."

"Listen, kid, I'm not stupid. The order says 'Susie Fish on Westridge'."

Charlie laughed. "Susie Fish? . . . The only Susie Fish here is a dog."

The man's face darkened with anger. "Y'know, I'm

damned tired of you spoiled brats playing pranks." His hands squeezed into fists.

"Go away!" Charlie slammed the door shut. He went back into the living room, and turned the TV volume up all the way. The insipid American Bandstand theme blasted over the angry insistent doorbell and the fist pounding the screen door. The end credits rolled. The show was over. No more Justine. Charlie's dick was soft again. "Stupid pizza asshole," he mumbled to himself.

After another minute, the knocking and ringing stopped. An "I Love Lucy" rerun came on. Charlie sighed. Ethel Mertz did nothing for him. He turned off the TV. He would have to forage through his father's closet for the Jayne Mansfield issue of Playboy. Jayne was sure-fire beat-off material. He went into his parents' bedroom.

He opened the closet. He knelt down to forage through the shoes and Life Magazines on the bottom of the closet. Jayne Mansfield was somewhere in that mess.

The whoop of a siren and a loudly clanging bell interrupted his feverish search. "What the hell?"

He ran to the window. An Oak Park City Fire Engine was parked in front of the house. Firemen in full gear scrambled off the truck. Charlie gasped. "Holy crap!"

He ran to the living room. He opened the front door. A tall muscular fireman walked briskly up the sidewalk. "Where's the fire?"

Normally, this would be the punch line to a bad joke, but neither Charlie nor the fireman could see the humor. "There's no fire here, sir," he stammered.

"What?" The fireman looked at him incredulously.

Charlie began to feel fear. First the pizza delivered to the wrong house and now a visit from the fire department. "I think somebody is playing a trick, sir."

"'A trick?" The tall man removed the heavy hat off his head. "Do you know that you can go to jail for a false alarm, kid?"

"But it wasn't me."

"Y'know, I remember you, kid. Don't think I don't. A couple of years ago I caught you and your buddy drawing dirty pictures on the old firehouse building. Remember that?"

Charlie was beginning to get angry. "I said it wasn't me."

"How do I know that, kid?"

"Take my word for it."

"I got kids pullin' this garbage on us at least once a week. And it always happens right around this time of day, when school gets out."

Celia's Oldsmobile turned into the driveway. A horrified expression was on her face. She rolled down the window. "Officer, what's going on here? This is my home!" she sputtered to the fireman.

He sauntered over to the car, his hands on his hips, a cynical look on his face. Charlie followed at a safe distance.

"Is this your son, ma'am?" asked the fireman.

"Yes, of course."

"Well, ma'am, it looks like your son may have decided to have a little fun today at the taxpayers' expense."

"No! I didn't! I told you that!" Charlie protested.

"What? I don't understand," she said to the fireman, ignoring Charlie's plea.

"Your son may have called in a false alarm."

"Oh my God! Oh my God!" Celia moaned and held her face.

"He's wrong! No! It wasn't me!" Charlie's heart was beating so fast that it felt like it was coming out of his chest.

"You shut up! How dare you!" she growled.

"I'm telling the truth!"

"You're a liar!"

The fireman backed away from the car. He displayed his palms in a polite gesture of neutrality. "Okay, ma'am. We're going. Just make sure this doesn't happen again."

"Don't worry, officer, it won't," she said this without taking her hate-filled eyes off her son.

The fireman turned to walk back to the truck. He grumbled and gestured to his men to climb back on the truck.

Celia Fish's face trembled with anger. "Wait till your father hears about this, Charles!"

"My father?" Charlie laughed bitterly. "This is all his fault!"

"What? What did you say?"

"You heard me the first time."

"I've had enough of your insane big mouth! You make no sense!"

"My father knows who that maniac is, and you know he knows, mother!"

"What maniac? You're the maniac! Keep your stupid abnormal mouth shut!"

A small white panel truck pulled up behind the fire engine. A sign on the truck's side said "City of Oak Park Animal Control." A light-skinned black man stepped out. His uniform was a khaki version of an Oak Park police uniform. He wore heavy elbow-length leather gloves. He walked past the fire-man and over to Celia's Olds. "Excuse me, ma'am." His voice was very deferential. "Is this the Fish residence?"

She looked up at the man. Her expression of panic and outrage quickly changed to a bright cordial smile. "Oh, hello, officer."

Charlie had never seen her offend a stranger. She always gave strangers extra special treatment and sometimes even the benefit of the doubt over him. The fireman was a prime example.

"Did you have a fire here, ma'am?" asked the man.

"No, we didn't." She stiffened.

"Can we help you, mister?" Charlie interrupted. Celia aimed an angry look at him.

"Do you folks have a dog?"

"Yes. Of course. Her name is Susie. Is there anything wrong, officer?"

"We've received a complaint, ma'am."

"A complaint?"

"I told you, mother. It's the crazy woman. She called the fire department and this guy, too."

"Be quiet, Charles. Can't you see that I'm talking to the officer?"

"May I see the animal, ma'am?"

"Certainly. She's in the backyard."

"Who complained, mister?" Charlie interrupted.

"I really can't give you that information. All I can say is that your animal bit someone."

"Th-that's ridiculous," Celia stammered. "Susie wouldn't hurt anyone. She's an itty-bitty fifteen-year-old poodle. She doesn't have any teeth to bite anyone."

Charlie felt a rush of fear. He ran up the driveway to the rear of the house. "Susie!" he called out.

He had grown up with the little dog. As ugly, old, and drooly as Susie was, Charlie loved her. He unlatched the backyard gate. "Susie! Come here, girl!"

He entered the backyard. The dog was nowhere to be seen. He looked in Celia's prized petunia beds. Sometimes the little animal liked to lay on the petunias. She wasn't there. "Susie! Where are you?" he called out.

He ran behind the garage, and almost tripped over a shovel. He picked the shovel up to toss it aside, but stopped. There was blood on the shovel's blade. Charlie looked down. The small funny neurotic creature that was once his pet was now a bloody clump of hair. The dog's head was nearly severed from its neck. Charlie clutched his gut and vomited.

"Charles, what's going on back there?" shouted Celia.

"Don't come over here, mother!" he choked and leaned against the garage wall. He sobbed.

The animal control officer peeked behind the garage. Shock registered on his face.

"Mister, don't let my mother see this," he sobbed.

The stranger nodded.

Charlie felt a murderous rage. He wanted to kill the maniac, and chop off her head with a shovel. He wanted to kill his own father.

• 1976 •

"YISGADAL V'YISKADASH SH'MAY RABO." Fifteen men stood in a circle in the center of Celia Fish's living room, a prayer *minyan*. The women, except for Celia in her wheelchair, all sat on folding chairs on the outskirts of the *minyan*, joining in the Kaddish chant.

The circle of men included Charlie, Uncle Sheldon Sternbaum, Uncle Nate Nosanchuk, several so-called friends of the family and cousins, and Charlie's old high school buddy, Howieschultz.

Even at age thirty, Charlie still called him "Howieschultz." Howieschultz looked every bit like the successful Hollywood lawyer that he was, in his three-piece khaki Brooks Brothers suit and tortoise-shell glasses. The good life had also packed an extra sixty pounds onto his once scrawny frame.

They were unlikely lifelong friends, but they had once shared tormentors. Korkis and Rothman used to call Howieschultz "the refloogee" because of his Auschwitz survivor parents.

Howieschultz led the mourning prayer. Although he had lost the sidelocks, the yarmulka, and all the other trappings of his Hasidic youth, he rushed through the Hebrew words of the Kaddish like a rabbinical scholar. The older men, mostly Reform Jews, rushed to keep up. Charlie faked it, moving his lips.

"*Ba'almo dee vroo heerosay . . .*" The mourners chanted Kaddish for Morris Fish. None could keep up with Howieschultz.

· 1961 ·

CHARLIE AND HOWIESCHULTZ were newsboys, part of the 6:00 A.M. gang that met at the rickety delivery shed behind Beck Cleaners, which had recently changed its name from Teck Cleaners, which had earlier been known as Heck Cleaners.

On a below-zero winter Saturday morning, the newsboys waited impatiently for the Detroit *Free Press* delivery truck to arrive. They huddled around a potbelly stove in the center of the dinky shed, passing Thermoses of hot chocolate, cracking dirty jokes, doing whatever was necessary to cope with the cold. The truck was over an hour late. For almost two days, the roads had been covered with a thick layer of ice, nearly impossible driving conditions even for a truck with snow chains.

Charlie was also late. The sidewalks were too slick to ride his bike. He pulled a little red wagon behind him, *Free Press* saddlebags folded inside it. He walked carefully, measuring each step. He had already fallen on his ass four times. He cursed under his breath and tried to accept the fact that his deliveries would probably take twice as long this morning and that his nuts could actually turn into snowballs and drop off.

As he approached the delivery shed, Charlie saw Howieschultz. He was kicking at one of the snowplow-created walls of snow that lined the alley behind Beck Cleaners. "Hey, whorehound!" Charlie shouted.

Howieschultz didn't respond with his usual "Hey, dickhead!" He kicked chunks out of the snow wall.

Charlie pulled a thin paperback out of his coat pocket and waved it proudly. "I got a Tijuana Bible, Howieschultz! A good one! Betty and Veronica doin' the do with Archie!"

"Fuck Betty and Veronica!" he shouted and rammed the snow wall with his shoulder, creating a mini-avalanche. A large chunk of ice-caked snow broke loose and fell on top of the small boy, knocking him to the ground and turning his black furry grizzly-bear parka polar-bear-white. "Shit! Cocksucker!" he screamed.

Charlie began to run, his feet scrambling on the ice and the little red wagon fishtailing behind. "Howieschultz! Are you okay? What's wrong?"

The scrawny boy pulled himself to his knees. He brushed the snow off his face and sidelocks. He hyperventilated with a rage that Charlie had never seen. "Ya wanna know what's wrong, Fish? It's my goddamn mother!" he shouted. "Can't keep her goddamn mouth shut!" He furiously slapped off the white powder from the front of his parka.

Charlie grabbed at his arm to help him to his feet. Howieschultz pushed him away. "Fuck off! I can do it myself, Fish." He pulled himself to a standing position. "Good old Yetta," he laughed bitterly. "Yetta the *Yenta*. She just can't resist bragging about her boy the honor roll genius! My old lady! Playing Mah-Jongg with shit-for-brains Rothman's old lady! . . . Yack yack yack! Mine Howard this! Mine Howard that! Mine Howard has all A's on his fucking report card! Yack yack yack!"

"So what? You should be proud of your grades. Let her brag."

"Yeah. Sure. Easy for you to say. What do you think Mrs. Big Ass Rothman does after hearing this news, Fish? Do you think she's happy? Especially since her sonny-boy bagged a couple of D's this semester. So, Mrs. Big Ass Rothman goes home, blows her stack, and she grounds her little prick son. Home by 8:00 P.M. on the weekends. So, David 'Crapface' Rothman and his simian pal, Korkis the Walking Armpit, did a real number."

"Did they jump you?"

Howieschultz stared deep into Charlie's eyes. Tears rolled down his face. "Look at this shit." He pulled a white envelope, folded into quarters, out of his pocket.

Charlie unfolded the envelope. Red crayon swastikas surrounded the block-letter words, "*Mockies*, Go Back To Auschwitz!"

"I found it this morning stuck in the screen door. Thank God my parents didn't see it."

Charlie opened the flap and looked inside the envelope. It was filled with cigarette ashes. He shook with rage.

His own mother made frequent remarks about "the greenhorns." "They're all filthy dirty! Unkempt. Their houses smell. I wouldn't take a drink of water in any of their houses."

His father would always respond, "They're Jews like us. But for the grace of God and the United States of America, we coulda wound up like them. You should be ashamed of yourself, Celia!"

Howieschultz snatched the envelope out of Charlie's hand, crumpled it in a ball, and ground it into the snow with his foot. "I'll kill 'em!"

"Bastards! . . . C'mon. Let's go talk to Joe Murphy."

"No Joe Murphy this time. It's my beef."

"What are *you* gonna do, Howieschultz?"

"My old man's got a can of gasoline in the garage. You can turn a lotta stuff into ashes with gasoline," he said this in a dead-quiet monotone.

Charlie trembled. He took Howieschultz's uncharacteristic killer demeanor very seriously. Howie was a *kibitzer*, a *tummeler*, and the life of the party, not a killer. "What's fucking up Rothman gonna do, Howieschultz? You're just gonna sink to his level."

"Do me a favor, Fish. Take my route today. Take my route book. I'll pay you extra." He removed a small spiral notebook from his pocket, gave it to Charlie, and stomped off before Charlie could accept or reject the added workload. "I gotta think, Fish," he called over his shoulder.

Charlie opened his mouth wide and swallowed down a

big gulp of icy air, trying to push his frustration and anger deep down into his bowels. He didn't run after his friend. He knew that Howieschultz wouldn't act on his threat. He had used the word "think."

When the *Free Press* delivery truck finally arrived, Charlie folded and loaded each newspaper into the little red wagon, creating an unwieldy mound of cylinders. He tied it all together with twine and hoped that his cargo wouldn't capsize. He was lucky that it was Saturday morning or else he'd be late for school.

Charlie carefully pushed the red wagon along the icy sidewalk placing both hands on the wagon's sides for stability. He was only barely aware of the cold and the four hours that passed as he delivered the papers for two routes. For the first time in his life, he thought about being Jewish, about Howieschultz's parents, about Nazis and Hitler and Auschwitz. He wondered how and if his own parents would've survived. Above all, he thought about David Rothman, a Jewish kid, drawing swastikas on an envelope.

To Charlie, Judaism and especially his own Bar Mitzvah were nothing more than meaningless jokes. "Today you are a man." He said that phrase aloud. That's what they tell a Bar Mitzvah boy. He didn't feel like a "man" at age thirteen. To Charlie, the envelope filled with cigarette ashes was his real Bar Mitzvah . . . at age fourteen. "Today you are a Jew, Charlie Fish."

From that day on, Charlie and Howieschultz would be forever linked. Bar Mitzvah boys.

• 1963 •

OAK PARK HIGH School students sat at the rows of long tables in the cafeteria according to social pecking order.

The fourth table in the lunchroom belonged to "the funny losers." They included Howieschultz, Charlie, and Joe Murphy, as well as "Metal Mouth" Felch, a very handsome kid with Buick–bumper-sized braces on his teeth, and "Porcupine" Cohen, a quill-haired wildman who wore sunglasses at night and was convinced that he had "Negro blood." "Porcupine" would "float" between the "loser" table and the black tables in the rear of the room. Black students from the post–World War Two quonset hut housing of nearby Royal Oak Township had been bused into the Oak Park school district since 1961. They made up twenty percent of the student body.

The third table belonged to the hoods, including Psycho Bobby Shapiro and Chris Korkis. Occasionally, Psycho Bobby would leave the hood table to sit with Joe Murphy. He had a healthy respect for Joe since their wrestling match, and the "funny losers" made him laugh.

At the funny loser table, Psycho Bobby and Joe Murphy giggled over the pornographic comics in a Swedish skin mag that Bobby bought from a "creep" at the Stone Burlesk in downtown Detroit.

The second table in the cafeteria was reserved for the jocks and student council brownnosers.

The first table in the lunchroom was reserved for "The

Preps," the school's "creme de la creme" fraternity. The Preps wore cashmere sweaters and drove Corvettes, T-Birds, or daddy's Caddies.

David Rothman was a newly initiated member. Not long after his humiliating gym class wrestling defeat, Rothman washed the VO5 out of his hair and combed it into a respectable collegiate style. He bought V-neck sweaters, and began getting good grades. He transformed himself into perfect "Prep" material, becoming preppier than the preppiest Prep. Instead of thanking Charlie for his turn-around, Rothman's bullying became subtler, more insidious. Social snobbery was his new weapon.

The prettiest girls sat at the Preps' table, including Judy Weinstein, the object of Charlie Fish's affection. She had only recently become David Rothman's girlfriend. He quietly watched Judy Weinstein and David Rothman. She was laughing at one of Rothman's jokes. Her smile broke his heart. As Rothman put his arm around her shoulder, he caught Charlie's gaze. He smirked and pulled her closer to him.

Judy Weinstein had been Charlie's first and only crush, his dreamgirl, since the day that they went to the eighth-grade Halloween party together and she let him kiss her cheek. Their friendship never blossomed because Judy's foot doctor father didn't approve of him. After all, he was a "gangster's son." Rothman would be an acceptable boyfriend in the eyes of Judy's father. Julius Rothman, David's father, was an osteopath, the portrait of respectability.

Charlie could hear the sound of Judy Weinstein's laughter. He loved how the dimples appeared in her cheeks when she laughed. "Look at those Prep assholes. What do they have that we don't?" muttered Charlie to anyone who would listen.

"They got all the fucking money in the world," muttered Howieschultz. Despite his perfect grades and orthodox demeanor, he had a mouth like a sewer. He was also the only one of Charlie's friends that was getting laid regularly. At night, Howieschultz would sneak his steady girlfriend, Rita Sue Baumgarten, into his house through the bedroom window. As long as he stayed on the honor roll and said his daily prayers, his parents would never question his locked door or the squeals and giggles coming from his bedroom.

"I'll tell ya the biggest difference between us and them fratboy daisies," said Joe Murphy. "They're organized."

"I'd like to play La Bamba on their faces," spat Psycho Bobby. He lobbed the remains of his Sloppy Joe "flying saucer-style" at the Preps' table. It narrowly missed Adam Green's Madras shirt and splattered against a tile wall. Adam Green flushed and turned his head, refusing to make eye contact with Psycho Bobby Shapiro or anyone else at the loser table. Although Green was six feet five inches tall and a star basketball player, Psycho Bobby intimidated him. Psycho Bobby and his tattoos intimidated everyone, except Joe Murphy.

"If it's a question of organization, let's fucking organize," said Howieschultz. He stood up and banged the lunch table with his fist.

"Yeah. We'll call ourselves 'The Shlongs' an' get sweatshirts that say 'The Shlongs,'" Joe Murphy guffawed.

"Yeah, we could all wear rubbers on our heads," laughed Metal Mouth Felch, who always carried one dried-out Trojan rubber in his wallet for "emergencies" that never happened. He was as lucky in love as he was handsome.

Everybody laughed, except Howieschultz. "No. We'll fucking call ourselves 'The Three Bs'—Booze, Broads, and Bagels."

Everyone stopped laughing.

"I like it." Charlie smiled.

"Hey, I ain't joinin' no pansy fraternity," said Psycho Bobby. "What will my bros in the Gypsy Clowns say?"

Psycho Bobby was the only Jewish member of a Hazel Park motorcycle club, the roughest motorcycle club in the metropolitan Detroit area.

"It doesn't have to be a fraternity. We don't want to wind up like those rich pussies. They think they're too cool to have fun. Booze, Broads, and Bagels will be about having fun, having parties, having girls. Why should pricks like Rothman have all the girls?" said Charlie.

"Exactly, Gefilte Fish," said Joe Murphy.

"Yeah, look at all those girls at that Prep table. They could be sitting at this table. They could be sitting on our faces," said Howieschultz.

"Yeah, I could stand to get laid," said Metal Mouth Felch.

Charlie stared at Judy Weinstein, her azure blue eyes, her lovely oval face. David Rothman gave her a light peck on the lips. She smiled at him, enjoying his attention. Charlie felt like crying.

"Let's do it," he said to his friends. "The Three Bs—Booze, Broads, and Bagels!"

"But, I don't like any of you motherfuckers," laughed Psycho Bobby.

"I say we buy some sweatshirts. Purple ones like that gang in Westside Story," said Metal Mouth Felch.

"Thas cool," mumbled the Porcupine, nodding behind his downtown shades.

"Okay," Psycho Bobby sighed with resignation. "Just sweatshirts. No frat boy bullshit."

"Fish and I can draw the club insignia. I'll draw the Broad. Fish can draw the Booze and the Bagel," said Joe Murphy. He lifted his leg and farted for emphasis. Howieschultz gave him "the finger." Everyone else at the "funny loser" table cursed, held their noses, scrambled out of their seats, and exited the lunchroom.

· 1976 ·

CHARLIE "RODE SHOTGUN" in Howieschultz's new black Cadillac Coupe De Ville convertible, a vehicle fit for a successful Los Angeles attorney. The Caddy barreled up Northwestern Highway, its top down.

When Howieschultz heard that Charlie's father had died, he drove the Caddy from L.A. to Detroit in a day and a half, only stopping for gas and burgers.

"Where the fuck are we going, Fish?" Howieschultz asked.

"I got unfinished business," said Charlie.

1976

Howieschultz

"I know you, man. You got that funny look in your eyes like you're gonna do something fucking nuts."

"I'm doing what I gotta do."

"Look, Fish, get the fuck outta Detroit. This revenge shit is a waste of time. Move to LA. I got an empty room in my house since divorce number two. I'll get you laid. I'll get you high. You got nothing keeping you here since Nancee split on ya."

This last comment hurt Charlie. He'd been divorced from Nancee for a year and he still felt bad about it. "Shut up and drive, Howieschultz."

"Fuck driving. Listen to me, Fish. I'm an attorney. Never underestimate the powers of a good shyster. We can fuck this jerk with the law."

"The law won't work with this guy." Charlie frowned and stared at the many large and small mirror-facade structures along Northwestern Highway. After the 1967 Detroit riots, many essential businesses and corporate offices deserted the once thriving downtown and moved twenty miles northwest to Southfield, dubbed "the new downtown."

"C'mon, Fish. Let me turn around. We'll go to this bar in Birmingham. Full of horny alcoholic divorcees. I'll get you laid and you can forget about this shit."

"I don't want to get laid. I'll take care of this mother-fucker myself. You don't have to get your hands dirty."

"I'm on your side, Fish. You know that. *Semper fratre* and all that shit. Who is this guy anyway?"

"A goddamn creep. Get ready to turn. The building is two blocks up. See the sign that says 'Carnegie Roosevelt and Associates'?"

"'Carnegie Roosevelt'?"

"It's a fake name. The creep thinks it's classy. Turn left into the parking lot."

Howieschultz's Caddy turned into the parking lot next to the mirror-facade one-story office building. He parked the car. There were other black Caddies in this lot. "I don't like this, Fish. Think before you do."

"I gotta do what I gotta do. If you're scared, drive away. No hard feelings. This is my nightmare, man." Charlie opened the door and stepped out.

"I'll wait."

"You don't have to, man." Charlie shut the passenger door, and walked toward the building, his fists clenched. He could see his own angry face in the mirrored wall of the Carnegie Roosevelt Building.

Charlie entered the building. Carnegie Roosevelt and Associates consisted mostly of one large fluorescent-lit room with an acoustic-tiled ceiling. The room was filled with several long tables. Shifty middle-aged fat guys in sweat-stained plaid sports jackets and a few long-haired twenty-year-old males in T-shirts and jeans sat at these tables and talked rapidly and loudly into telephones. They were all making cold calls, a classic boilerroom sales operation. Everything from scrap metal to cheapo real estate was being sold over the phones.

At 350 pounds, Otto Bloom, the supervisor, was the fattest fat guy of the bunch. He waddled back and forth between the long tables, the stub of a vile unlit Italian stick-cigar jammed in the corner of his mouth, as he barked orders, cursed, or spewed the punchlines of bad dirty jokes at the others. "Hey, Ed! Am I payin' ya to talk boojy-boojy to your ol' lady? Make some goddamn calls already. Hey, Shtummy! What did I tell ya? Get that dogshit look offa your face when you're talkin' to the customer. Give her a nice big smile. It'll help you make the goddamn sale. Yeah. That's more like it. Now you're bee-yoo-tee-ful."

Charlie knew most of the middle-aged fat guys in the room. When he was in his early twenties, he had a summer job in Krantz's boilerroom at the old Livernois Avenue location in northwest Detroit. He'd make cold calls to white homeowners in "changing neighborhoods"—blockbusting.

He could still hear the old spiel in his head. "Hello, Mrs. Pokorny, this is Mr. Brown from C. Roosevelt Realty. Would you like cash for your home now?"

As Charlie entered the room, Otto Bloom looked up, gave him a high sign, and flashed him a yellow-toothed grin. "Charlie Charlie Charlie. I heared about Morris. Your old man, he was a class act, a great card player. Why the fuck did he do it? Why the fuck did he do it?"

"*He* didn't do it, Otto."

"Whuh you mean by that?" There was a glazed confused expression on Otto Bloom's fat sweaty face.

"Is Krantz here?"

Otto pointed toward a closed office door. "He's in there, but he's on the muscle today, kiddo. You know how Lowell can get. Come back tomorrow."

"Thanks, Otto." Charlie turned and walked to the closed office door.

"Hey! Din't you hear me? I sez he was busy, kid!"

Charlie flung open the office door and entered.

∵

KRANTZ'S office was a tasteful contrast to the boiler-room. His wife Florence was an interior decorator, and her "moderne" imprint was evident. The dominant color in the office was white: Krantz's plush leather executive chair, the three leather visitor chairs, and the walls. Krantz sat behind a sleek glass and chrome desk. He was embroiled in a heated phone conversation. He looked up at Charlie, an irritated expression on his face. He held up a finger, gesturing Charlie to wait. Krantz wore an expensive English-tailored navy blue suit. He looked like any Fortune 500 executive—only his white shirt and matching white tie revealed his Hastings Street origins. He resumed his phone conversation. "I tole ya, Ben, that cigar order you sent me was inferior crap. What do you think I am? A stupid *goy*? I wanted Cuesta Reys, not these Tampa goddamn factory seconds!"

Charlie noticed a blackboard with white chalk writing in a corner of the office. A large chalk triangle was on the board. Above the triangle was a title: "Super Pyramid." The triangle contained rows of squares, a scribbled name inside each square. Charlie walked to the blackboard. He could make out his father's name in a bottom square. It had only barely been erased.

"Ben, you send a goddamn truck out here in one hour flat to pick these boxes of shit up today. You don't want to piss me off! One hour or I play nick-nack-paddy-wack on your fat ass! You hear me, Ben?" Krantz slammed down the phone.

He took a deep breath and glared up at Charlie. He forced a thin smile. "What can I do you for, Butch? You come here to apologize?"

Charlie rapped his knuckles against the blackboard. "What is this? What's my father's name doing on here? I know about these pyramid bullshit scams! You pull in a bunch of suckers and sell them shares in nothing, and the suckers pull in other suckers, etcetra, etcetra!"

Krantz's face turned red. "This ain't none of your business, Butch."

"You need to front a lot of money to play this pyramid scam, don't you, Mr. Krantz? My father was one of your suckers!"

Krantz lurched out of his chair. "It's multilevel marketing. Legit. I don't scam anyone. These names on that board are doctors, lawyers, high-class people. Hell, I got my own money riding on this. Listen, this is my private business. I don't want to talk about it." Krantz was almost hyperventilating.

The office door opened and a large red-headed man's face peered inside. It was an ugly mashed-in boxer's face. His nose consisted of two nostrils. "Everything all right in here, Lowell?"

"It's Morris's kid, Red." Krantz nodded at the big man.

"Okay, Lowell. I'll be outside the door." Red gave Charlie a dirty look and shut the door.

"Look, Butch, you're barking up the wrong tree an' I'm busy. We can talk about this some other time. I'll take you to dinner at my club."

"My old man was into you big-time, wasn't he, Mr. Krantz?"

"Now I'm gonna have to ask you to leave."

Charlie had no intention of leaving. He folded his arms across his chest and glared at Krantz. "I want answers and I want them now." Charlie pulled his father's I.O.U. out of his pants pocket and slapped it onto Krantz's desk, nearly crackling the glass top.

"Get out of my office. I'm serious." Krantz grabbed the paper, crumpled it into a wad, and threw it at Charlie, hitting his cheek.

Charlie screamed "You thieving motherfucker!" He

pushed Krantz hard in the chest, sending him sprawling onto the floor. The big white chair smashed against the back wall.

Red stormed into the office.

"What the fuck?!" Red grabbed Charlie and slammed him against the nearest wall and kicked him in the balls.

Charlie fell to the floor, and curled into a fetal position. Red kicked him in the face. Charlie tasted blood in his mouth.

"That's enough, Red!" Krantz climbed back to his feet. The thug drew his foot back for another kick, stopped, then stepped away from Charlie.

Howieschultz entered the office. He looked down at Charlie. Every part of Howieschultz's body trembled.

"Who the fuck are you?" shouted Red.

"I-I'm an attorney, and th-this is my friend."

"If you're smart, you'll get your dumb friend out of here, lawyer," said Lowell Krantz.

"Yes. Of course," said Howieschultz. He bent down to help Charlie to his feet.

Howieschultz steered Charlie toward the open office door. "Are you fucking crazy? Let's get out of here!" he whispered harshly to Charlie.

Krantz shouted after them. "You listen to me, boy, an' listen good! I didn't kill your old man! This is the last time I say this!"

As they exited, Charlie turned and spit a bloody phlegm wad onto Krantz's white carpet. "You killed my father. I know you did."

"You come back here an' I'll kill you," hissed Krantz.

∵

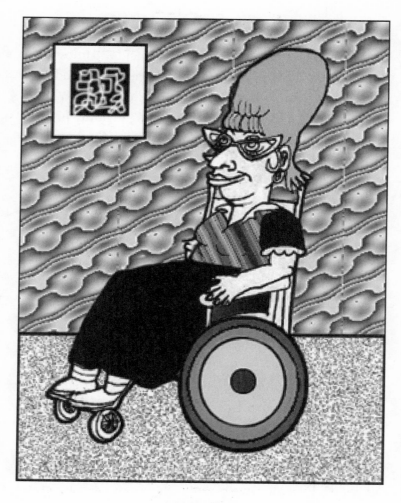

Celia Fish

sitting shiva

•••

CHARLIE entered his mother's apartment at almost three a.m. He was sloshed. Charlie and Howieschultz had been passing joints and a bottle of Old Bushmill's Irish Whiskey back and forth for several hours. Anything to numb his rage.

All the lights in the apartment were off. Charlie felt his way through the living room. He stumbled over his own booze-heavy feet, and grabbed onto the nearest wall.

"Charles." His mother's voice startled him.

He fumbled along the wall for a light switch. He flicked it on. In the center of the living room, Celia Fish was sitting in her wheelchair, perched upright and very much awake. She was wringing her hands, a nervous habit that always preceded a tirade. "Where have you been, Charles?"

"I had to run an errand," he half-lied.

"What errand?"

"Don't worry about it."

"What do you mean 'don't worry'? I am worried. You've been gone for hours. I didn't know where you were. You were supposed to be here."

"I'm sorry, mother."

"Do you think that 'sorry' is supposed to make everything all right? Everyone was asking about you. I was embarrassed. Was I supposed to tell them that you went on a joyride? Was I supposed to tell them that you have no respect for your father?" Her voice quavered.

"Mother, you're working yourself up. Please stop."

"Your father was right all along. He said that, as soon as he was gone, you'd knife me in the back."

"You've had a long day, mother. I know that you don't mean what you're saying."

"Like hell I don't. Your father may not have had a formal education, but he did have common sense. He pegged you right."

"Common sense"—these words rubbed Charlie raw. He laughed bitterly, through his whiskey haze.

"So now he's laughing. I'm dying inside and he's laughing." Tears rolled down her face. "You left me here all alone, and those calls started again."

He felt a jolt of fear. "What calls?"

"*Her* calls. Who else?"

"What are you talking about, mother? That maniac's been dead for years!"

"Who says?" Her face darkened with a vindictive anger.

"You yourself told me this five or six years ago."

"I never said that. I had to take the phone off the hook. Do you see?"

Charlie saw that the receiver was lying face-up on the lamp table. His face flushed. His legs felt wobbly. Conflicting thoughts rushed through his head. His mother was either telling the truth, or it was another one of her elaborate ploys for attention. Throughout the years, Celia Fish's sense of drama was almost ingenious—her greatest gift and most blatant curse. Whenever she felt neglected, she would do whatever was necessary to place herself in the center of the spotlight. Charlie refused to allow himself to get pulled into her act. "You're just upset and tired, mother."

"Why do you keep saying that?"

Charlie walked behind the wheelchair and pushed it toward the bedroom.

"What do you think you're doing?"

"You're going to bed."

"No, I'm not!"

Charlie wheeled her into the bedroom.

"Damn your hide! Didn't you hear me?"

"I don't want you to get sick, mother."

"So now you care, huh? Well, it's too late! You care more about gallivanting with your lousy friends than you do about me."

"That's not true." He tried to control his anger, but she was pushing every button.

"Do you know that I had to lie today? I had to tell everybody that you had business at the funeral home. You made a liar out of me."

"You created your own lie, mother. What's the difference?"

Celia pulled her body into a ramrod straight position. "And what does that mean?"

"My father ate his gun." These words blurted out of Charlie. He knew they were the wrong as soon as he said them.

Celia's face turned bright red. She hurled her body out of the wheelchair and slapped Charlie across his already sore mouth. "Never say anything bad about your father! You traitor! Get out of my house! I'm through with you! Get out!" she screamed.

Her flash of violence shook him. He displayed his palms in a gesture of surrender. "I'm sorry, mother. I hurt as bad as you do."

"Get out!" she shrieked. "I don't know what I did to deserve you!"

The intensity of her voice caused him to stumble backwards. He edged his way toward the bedroom door. "I'll be outside, sleeping in my car." He said this quietly.

"I don't care what you do," she spat at him.

Charlie shook his head in frustration and exited the apartment, slamming the door behind him.

"The Bumblebee" was parked in front of the apartment building. He opened the passenger door and pulled a lever next to the front seat. The seat flopped back into a semi-reclining position. Charlie slid his body onto the impromptu bed, but there was no sleep in him. The whiskey had given him no relief, only a headache. Words and images of the prior twenty-four hours flashed randomly and painfully through his head: his mother's trembling finger of accusation, his father's nearly erased name inside the chalk pyramid on Lowell Krantz's blackboard, the maniac's telephone whisper.

Charlie sobbed. He couldn't stop.

•••

third day
of shiva

· 1962 ·

CHARLIE WALKED DOWN Westridge Street toward his home. He was able to con Mrs. Scoggins, the school nurse, into believing that he was sick, which was fairly easy because he had puked up Salisbury steak dangerously close to the brightly polished cordovan crepe-soled shoes of Mr. McGruder the tight-ass cafeteria monitor. Neither Mrs. Scoggins nor Mr. McGruder knew that puking at will was one of Charlie's hidden talents. He did what he had to do to avoid taking the algebra midterm exam that afternoon. Charlie hated algebra. It had no purpose in his life; however, the night before the test, he promised himself that he would stay up late and cram. Instead he stayed up late, crept into his parents' living room, and watched back-to-back Edward G. Robinson gangster movies—"Brother Orchid" and "Bullets or Ballots"—on CKLW's Million Dollar Midnight Movies.

As Charlie approached his parents' house, he saw his dad's car parked in the driveway. Morris Fish rarely came home before 7 p.m. He must be sick, thought Charlie; one of his annual malaria attacks courtesy of the Solomon Islands.

Charlie would have to come up with a suitable lie

explaining why he was getting out of school early; but his father always knew when he was "goldbricking."

He entered the house. "Dad?" he called out. There was no answer.

He peeked into the living room. His father wasn't in his napping spot, on the plastic-covered couch.

He went to his parents' bedroom. There was no one in the room.

His father wasn't in the bathroom either.

He went to the kitchen. No one there.

Charlie was beginning to worry. He descended the steps to the basement. He entered the rec room. Only the tarp-covered pool table was there.

He heard a muffled voice from Delphine the maid's tiny bedroom. The door was shut. He knew that, since his mother was out on errands or social obligations, Delphine had to be with her. He pressed his ear to the door. The muffled voice belonged to his father. Charlie touched the doorknob, then stopped. His father and his mother never entered Delphine's bedroom. He wondered why his father was whispering.

He quietly climbed up the steps toward the kitchen.

His legs trembled as he approached the canary-yellow telephone mounted on the daisy-pattern wallpapered kitchen wall. He gently, slowly lifted the phone receiver off the hook. Feelings of terror and curiosity clashed inside him as he placed the receiver to his ear.

He heard his father's voice, and recognized the other voice: a schizo voice that fluctuated between a hysterical bloody explosion of laughter and an ominous whisper.

"Money is tight right now, Antoinette," said Morris Fish. Antoinette, an ordinary enough name, thought Charlie.

"Bullshit. You can't hold out on me like this, you goddamn Jew!" she hissed.

"You know I don't like you callin' me that."

"I don't give a fuck. That goddamn Jew baby doctor is on my ass again. I need cash."

"Okay. Okay. I'll pay him. I toldya I would, for godsakes."

"You goddamn better. It's your kid."

"You don't know that an' neither do I. Hell, it could be Tony Scotto's kid."

"Don't give me that crap, Morris. It ain't been nobody but you for the past year. An' you know it too. Goddamn it."

"I can't keep you in fuckin' money, Antoinette. Mebbe you oughta cut down on the booze, cigarettes, an' restaurant food."

Charlie repeated the name "Antoinette" inside his head. Like "Marie Antoinette, the whore who got her head chopped off in the French Revolution."

"*You're* tellin' *me* to cut down, you sonofabitch? You should talk. Maybe if you'd cut down on the cards and ponies . . . ," she screamed.

"Now you're startin' to sound like Celia with the nagging . . . grind grind grind."

The sound of his mother's name coming from his father's mouth sickened Charlie.

"I ain't nothin' like the Queen Bitch. I give you all the action you can handle. She don't give you shit. An' I still look pretty damn good at my age. I make sure of it. An' you like it,

Morris, don't you? You like that my tits don't sag, that my belly's still flat. But it comes at a price. It all takes money. The beautician. The pretty clothes. The makeup. You wouldn't like it if I let myself go like the Queen Bitch, would you?"

"I tole you not to call her that, Antoinette."

"I don't care. She and that overgrown spoiled brat of yours got everything. Me an' your baby got nothin'!"

"Shut the fuck up! You hear me?"

Charlie wanted to scream into the phone, but clamped his jaws tight. He wanted to hear it all. He wanted to know how far her reign of terror against his mother would go. He wanted to know how big a bastard his father was.

"You hear *me*, Morris! How 'bout I take a walk on you, an' you never see me or the kid again? How'd you like them beans?"

Morris Fish sighed, then mumbled. Charlie couldn't understand the words.

"I didn't hear you. What did you say to me?" Her voice was a high-decibel shriek.

"I sez, I wouldn't want you to walk on me." These words were quiet, serious, worried.

"Okay, then we know where we stand. I got expensive tastes. I admit it. That's somethin' we both gotta live with. You like the way I look an' the way I make you feel. Nobody treats you like I do. That's why you gotta divorce that Queen Bitch once an' for all."

"I can't. You know she's sick."

" 'Sick?' I wish she'd goddamn die!"

"I sez, knock it off, Antoinette!"

"I'll shut up when she's dead. You keep tellin' me she's gonna die soon an' she never does. If eleven years in that TB hospital didn't kill her, nothin' will. She'll outlive us all. Maybe if I fuckin' kill her. Sneak into that house and cut her into a million pieces! How'd you like that?"

"You dirty cunt! You stay away from her an' my kid!"

"Oh, so now you hear me. Okay. Good. Now listen, I need eight hundred bucks for that Jew doctor. You're gonna pay or else," her voice hissed.

Charlie could hear his father breathing heavily into the phone.

"Okay. Okay. Okay. I'll get the goddamn money, but I'm gonna have to get a loan from somewhere."

"Bull-fucking-shit!" She hung up with a click that hurt Charlie's ear. His heart hurt worse. He hated his father. He knew that, despite the tough guy facade, Morris Fish was a weak man. He suspected that his father agreed with that "twisted psycho whore" and wanted his mother to get sicker and die.

Charlie heard his father trudging up the basement steps. He quickly hung up the phone, opened the door to the nearby broom closet, slid inside the narrow space, and closed the door. A fearful sweat rolled down his face.

• 1976 •

CHARLIE JOLTED AWAKE. The handbrake lever jammed into his backbone. He felt like he had ten pounds of wet clay inside his brain. His breath and farts had fogged up the Bumblebee's windshield. He rolled down the driver's window.

How would he survive another day of dealing with relatives and strangers? How would he survive another day of dealing with the demons of his past, present, and future?

Charlie stared at his Spiro Agnew watch, a birthday gift from Joe Murphy. It was a little after 7:00 A.M. His Aunt Beatrice had arrived; her Olds 98 was parked across the street. Charlie groaned, stretched, and flung open the Bumblebee's driver door. He stumbled out of the car. The air was humid; typical Michigan end-of-the-summer nastiness.

He walked toward his mother's apartment building. He wanted to go home, even though home was a downtown Detroit Gladstone Avenue roach trap.

He opened the apartment's front door and clenched his teeth in anticipation of his aunt's bad attitude.

As he entered, Aunt Beatrice peered out of the tiny kitchen area. Her face was twisted into a self-righteous scowl. "Did you have a good night's sleep, Charles?"

"I love you too, Aunt Beatrice," Charlie mumbled as he headed for the bathroom to take a whiz and "a Polish shower"—a little water splashed on the pits.

"There's a sink full of dishes. It wouldn't kill you to help me. It's the *shvartza's* day off."

Charlie bristled and turned toward his aunt. "You know I hate that word."

"What word?" she smiled meanly at him. Charlie and

Aunt Beatrice had many screaming arguments at family dinners about her racist comments. Nothing made him angrier than bigoted Jews.

"I don't want to fight with you today." He shook his head in disgust and resumed his walk to the bathroom.

"Where are you going? Your mother is sound asleep. Don't wake her up."

"Do I have your permission to take a piss, Aunt Beatrice?" he muttered.

She fumed. "I won't have any of your potty mouth."

"The potty sounds pretty good to me right now." He smiled to himself and shut the bathroom door behind him.

•••

CHARLIE entered his mother's apartment kitchen. It was more a nook than a kitchen. There was barely enough room for him and his aunt. She was a large, yet attractive, middle-aged woman. If Elizabeth Taylor were six feet tall and 220 pounds, she'd be Aunt Beatrice.

The kitchen sink was filled with suds. His aunt ignored him. She zealously attacked Celia's china and silverware with a Brillo pad. Charlie grabbed a dishrag. She passed a wet plate to him. He dried it off and put it in the rubber-coated wire rack with all the other plates, bowls, and platters. She passed another plate to him, establishing a work rhythm.

"Don't break any of your mother's good china," she said quietly. The china and silverware were his mother's last remnant of luxurious living.

"Can I ask you a question, Aunt Beatrice?"

"No time for chit-chat. This place is a holy mess. People will be here at nine," she grumbled.

"This is important."

She sighed heavily, set a turkey platter onto the dish rack, and turned to face him, her hands on her beefy hips. "What is it?"

"Do you remember that crazy woman my father was involved with?"

Her face turned scarlet. "You should be ashamed of yourself bringing up that trash at a time like this!"

"My father would sometimes confide in you, Aunt Beatrice."

"Rarely."

"Did he ever say that I have a brother?"

The relish dish she was scrubbing bobbled in her hands and almost crashed to the floor. She turned to Charlie, a scowl on her face. "Are you insane, Charles?"

"Don't you think I have a right to know? Especially now that my father is gone?"

"Be quiet. You'll wake your mother."

"Tell me, Aunt Beatrice."

"All right," she sighed. "I'll say this once and we'll never have this discussion again. I loved your father, but he was a fool. A fool with a soft heart. That wasn't his baby. I know at least three men at your father's card club who were seeing her. She's nothing more than a common prostitute who was using him to get money. She was bleeding your father dry.

You're an only child; no brothers, no sisters . . . period. Okay? Are you satisfied?"

"No, I'm not satisfied. What other men was she seeing, Aunt Beatrice?"

"None of your business. I'm not a gossip."

"I need to know the truth."

"Let my brother lie in peace, Charles!" Her eyes filled with tears.

"I can't."

"Did you hear what I said? I don't want your mother catching wind of this conversation." Tears rolled down her face.

Charlie had seldom seen his Aunt Beatrice cry. She was the strongest member of the family. "Yes, Aunt Beatrice," he said quietly.

She turned the kitchen sink water knob with a jerk and hot water blasted out of the faucet. The rushing sound drowned out the possibility of any further conversation between them. She furiously washed dishes. Charlie reluctantly dried each dish as it was passed to him.

•••

DURING the early afternoon, Charlie tired of talking to his relatives. He locked himself in his mother's bedroom and watched her dinky black-and-white portable TV. Bill Kennedy was hosting the afternoon movie. Kennedy was a former Hollywood B-picture actor who knew the behind-the-scenes ins and outs of every Warner Brothers and MGM

picture from the 1930s and 1940s. He never failed to titil-
late, inform, or aim a sour grapes jibe at Tinseltown. As a
boy, Charlie would fake illnesses to stay home from school
to watch Bill Kennedy, especially if he was showing a Bogie,
Cagney, Edward G. Robinson, or John Garfield gangster
flick. On this afternoon, Kennedy was showing "Mr.
Skeffington," a Bette Davis–Claude Rains tearjerker that
always struck a nerve in Charlie, despite its total hokiness.
Bette Davis played a selfish faded beauty, and Claude Rains
played her faithful Jewish husband who was blinded by the
Nazis.

There was a sharp knock on the bedroom door. "Nobody
home," Charlie mumbled.

"Open up, Gefilte Fish! It's the FBI! You're busted, you
filthy commie!" boomed Joe Murphy's wrestler-voice.

Charlie scrambled off the bed. He opened the door, and
there was Joe Murphy and his ear-to-ear goofus grin. "Look
what the cat drug in, man," said Joe, as Darla Murphy
poked her head out from behind her brother's muscle-
bound body.

"Hi, Charlie," she said quietly, demurely.

"Darla," he gasped. He hadn't seen her in several years.
A gamut of emotions surged through him: joy, pain, sadness, regret, lust, anger—all rushing from his head to his
heart to his gut to his dick, then back to his head and on and
on, in no particular order.

She smiled sheepishly at him, moved past her brother,
and hugged Charlie. He squeezed her as tight as could. He
still loved her. He'd always love her.

"I'm so sorry," she whispered in his ear. He felt her warm lips.

"It's been too long," he whispered back.

"I'll let you two kids get reacquainted. There's some pastrami out in the living room with my name on it." Joe Murphy shut the bedroom door, leaving Charlie and his sister alone.

After a couple more minutes, Darla gently pulled back from the hug. They stared into each others' eyes. Although he loved her sky blue eyes, they always scared him a little. They seemed to stare far beyond him, to a place that he'd never reach.

She stepped back from him. In four years she had endured childbirth, two busted marriages, heroin, methadone, and the looney bin; all had taken a physical toll. Charlie was shocked and tried not to show his true feelings. Darla was only thirty-five years old and her body sagged like an old woman's. Deep lines etched her face, dark pouches sagged under her eyes, and her once-radiant ash blonde hair was as brittle and dry as straw. He could smell the cheap, sickeningly sweet perfume that only barely masked her body odor.

She smiled at him. Her smile was still beautiful. She looked him up and down. "You still look good."

"So do you," he lied.

Her smile vanished. Her eyes filled with tears. "No, I don't."

"To me, you'll always look good," he lied again.

She giggled like a little girl and flopped down on the bed.

Her flabby breasts and belly bounced. She smiled seductively and parted her legs slightly. "C'mere. Sit next to me," she cooed.

He wanted to vomit as he lowered his body next to her. He remembered the way she used to be.

• 1957 •

CHARLIE WAS ELEVEN. Darla was sixteen and pregnant. It was Christmas morning. He was in the Murphys' basement bathroom, feeling the full effects of wolfing down at least three pounds of Hershey bars. Gorging on chocolates was a Murphy family Christmas morning tradition. Charlie sat on the toilet to take a long leisurely shit. He thumbed through Joe Murphy Sr.'s latest issue of Argosy Magazine, a monthly anthology of cheesy "true" tales of adventure. The illustrations of stacked scantily-clad women in peril held his interest. He had a boner.

The bathroom door opened. He forgot to lock it. The magazine slipped out of his hand and fell to the floor. Darla Murphy poked her head inside the bathroom. She had the most beautiful face that he had ever seen: bright blue eyes, round dimpled cheeks, soft full red lips, and daisy yellow hair cut in Dutch-girl bangs. She smiled and stared straight at his boner. "Sorry." She shut the door.

He was horrified. Twenty minutes passed before he had the courage to leave the bathroom and make a quick escape out the back door.

For weeks afterward, Joe Murphy didn't let Charlie forget his humiliation. "My sis says you got a big one, Fish!"

Charlie was in love with his best buddy's sister and had to keep it to himself.

• 1976 •

DARLA WAS SOUND asleep on Charlie's mother's bed. She snored loudly. Saliva ran down both corners of her mouth. He sat on the edge of the bed, staring down at her. He felt a deep sadness. He wondered what would've happened if she had wound up with him years ago. He wondered if she still would've freaked out and ended up on the streets, and in Ypsi State Hospital.

Charlie got up from Celia's bed. He gently placed a pillow under Darla's head and covered her with a blanket. He lightly kissed her cheek and left the bedroom.

She made her choices and he made his.

• 1971 •

ALTHOUGH CHARLIE WENT to bed early, the downtown Detroit summer night was too muggy and noisy for sleep. He heard gunshots from Woodward Avenue. He heard the alky next door hacking hunks of bloody phlegm into the toilet. Even if the night were quieter and cooler, sleep still would be difficult. His fold-down Murphy bed was an uncomfortable mess with a huge camel-hump of wadded-up old newspapers stuffed inside a pizza-sized hole that was in the center of the mattress. Every time he'd roll over the hump, he'd hear the loud crunching and crinkling of paper.

An insistent knock on the apartment door jolted him into an upright position. He hadn't had a visitor in weeks. "Who is it?" he called out.

There was no answer

It could've been anyone. The apartment building's front door latch had been broken for weeks. The landlord couldn't give a shit about even minimal maintenance. Neighborhood whores, junkies, winos, crazies, and gang thugs hung out in the stairwells and corridors. A month earlier, Charlie's apartment door was kicked down while he was at work, and his portable TV and one ounce of shitty Indiana weed was ripped off. As a signature of their dirty work, the creeps had sliced a hole in his mattress and pulled out the stuffing. A trail of piss had led from the closet-sized bathroom to the center of the Mickey Mouse throw-rug on the center of the one-room apartment's floor. The place still smelled of piss, no matter how much disinfectant he used.

The knocking resumed, louder.

"Get the fuck outta here! I gotta fucking gun here!" Charlie bellowed.

"Charlie, it's me!" screamed a frantic female voice. "It's Darla."

The fear left him. He scrambled out of bed. He was bare-assed naked. He pulled on a ratty pair of gray sweatpants.

"I'm coming!" he shouted, as he lurched toward the door. He opened the door and there she was.

"I'm sorry," she sobbed. "It's so late." She entered. Tears ran down her cheeks. Her face was flushed, a bright pinkish color from crying. Charlie felt ashamed that he found her so attractive, especially in her state of upset. Besides being the object of his deepest secret desires, she was his friend, the married sister of his best buddy.

Charlie had always been crazy about her. Darla had never visited his apartment without her brother Joe. Everything about her was soft and lovely. "Darla, are you okay?"

"Ernie hit me again—the prick," she sobbed.

Charlie could never understand why she always ended up with brutish know-nothing assholes. Ernie Nichols, husband number three, was an alcoholic rich kid professional speedboat racer.

"Look at my face, Charlie." She pulled back her silky blonde hair to reveal a bruise on her cheek. "I walked out on his ass, got in my car, got on the expressway, and I didn't know where the hell I was driving, but I kept going until I wound up in downtown Detroit. Automatic pilot. I got lost, I got scared, then I remembered where you lived. So, here I am."

"This place is a dump, but you can stay as long as you like."

"I don't care about that. I'm just glad to see a friendly face." Darla kissed his cheek. She smelled like fresh peaches. Everything about her reminded him of peaches; soft, round, yellow, and pink. She took off her blue jean jacket. Her too-small Grateful Dead T-shirt showed off the roundness of her breasts. The low-slung hip-hugger jeans revealed her velvety tummy. Charlie almost swooned, but tried his best to hide it.

"Do you have anything to drink?" she asked.

"I got a bottle of Jack."

"Great. Let's get fucked up. I need it."

"Okay," said Charlie. As much as he loved Darla, there was an aggression, a savagery about her nature that both scared and excited him. Charlie went to the fridge and pulled out a half-filled fifth of Jack Daniels.

She sat on the threadbare couch. Charlie placed the bottle and two empty Peter Pan peanut butter jars on the orange crate coffee table. He sat on a folding chair facing the couch and poured sourmash into the jars.

"Why are you all the way over there, Charlie? After all these years, you can't be afraid of me," she said with a sexy pout.

"No," he stammered, got out of the chair, and sat on the couch.

"Don't be such a stranger, Charlie Fish." She scooted close to him. They were thigh-to-thigh. His heart jumped nervously. She lit a joint and extended it to him. "Have some," she cooed.

He took it. The end of the joint was wet from her lips. He put it in his mouth and tasted her.

Darla smiled, crossed her legs, and draped them over his lap. She reclined on the couch. "I've always felt relaxed around you, Charlie. That's a supreme compliment." She closed her eyes.

Several moments of quiet passed. Charlie worked up the nerve to stare down at her body. Her T-shirt displayed her hard nipples. Her soft pink stomach undulated with each breath. He couldn't take his eyes off her. She opened her eyes, and caught him. "I'm getting fat, don't you think?" she said. "Ernie calls me a fat pig."

"I think you're beautiful." Charlie stammered.

She smiled and held his hand. She lightly squeezed his hand. Her palm felt soft, slightly moist. "You're only saying that to make me feel better."

"I'm saying it because I love you." These words blurted out of him. He immediately felt ashamed.

Her face turned an emotional shade of red. She smiled sweetly at him, reached up, put her hands on the back of his neck, and pulled him down toward her. He moved back slightly, then surrendered. Their lips met softly, then electrically. She moaned. She opened her mouth. He tasted the bittersweet Jack Daniels on her tongue. Every part of his body was on fire. He placed his hand flat on her bare tummy. She gasped. He almost came in his pants.

"I love you, Darla," he whispered urgently in her ear.

She pulled away from him. "Don't say that word. Please."

A slightly hurt expression appeared on his face.

"Words are never enough, Charlie." She smiled and reached underneath his shirt. She playfully rubbed her hands on his chest. "I've always wanted to feel your curlies," she giggled. "Feel my curlies, too." She unsnapped the top button of her jeans and slid his hand inside. "Ooh," she moaned.

His hand moved down the softness of her belly to the wetness of her pussy.

"Do you like my pussy, Charlie Fish?"

"I love your pussy, Darla Murphy."

"Oh my God!" she groaned loudly, and grabbed desperately at his sweatpants, pulling it down past his knees. She rolled onto her side, placed her warm soft hand on his stiff prick, and gently stroked it. "I've always wanted you."

⁘

CHARLIE woke up at 3:00 A.M. He was sprawled out on the couch alone. "Darla?" he said this more to himself.

He could hear her voice coming from the tiny kitchen. It was a whisper. Charlie walked quietly to the kitchen and peeked in. Darla sat flat on the floor and was talking on the phone. Tears flowed down her face. Her words were urgent, heartfelt. Charlie thought about entering the kitchen to offer some comfort to her, but he froze.

"Yes, babe," she said to the phone. "I know. I know you're sorry. You're always sorry, but we can't go on like this . . . I can't tell you where I am . . . no, I'm at a friend's. A girl-friend."

Charlie felt a stab of pain at her lie.

"Babe, you always tell me that you're gonna get help, then you always slide back. It never lasts and I wind up being your whipping boy. I can't fucking take it . . . don't ask me that! I don't want to answer you. You know the answer to that question. No! . . . do you know how helpless I feel? I'm trapped. I feel like a goddamn junkie when it comes to you. I have to get clean, but I can't. I want to. I want to get clean. You know that," she sobbed.

Charlie walked back to the couch. He sat down hard. He was confused. He took a Kool cigarette from Darla's pack on the orange crate table. He hadn't smoked a cigarette in months. He lit the Kool and dragged deeply. The mentholated smoke streaming down his throat was a comfort. He began to regret his feelings toward her. He felt shame for screwing a married woman. His Fifties upbringing and his own father's adulteries were never far from his thoughts. He reclined on the couch and shut his eyes.

∵

WHEN Charlie woke up again. It was 8:00 A.M. Darla was gone.

He wasn't surprised.

• 1976 •

WHEN CHARLIE ENTERED the apartment living room, he heard laughter, genuine laughter, for the first time in days. Relatives, neighbors, and family friends were clustered by the couch. Charlie moved toward the group. A handsome, well-groomed man in his late twenties sat next to Celia. He wore a well-tailored khaki safari suit. At first, Charlie didn't recognize him, then he remembered. This man was at his father's funeral, the stranger who had the argument with the cemetery attendant. A TV table was set up in front of the stranger. He was rapidly and deftly shuffling a deck of cards, more like a magician than a card sharp. He was doing close-up magic. Everyone smiled at his antics and snappy patter, even Charlie's mother and Aunt Beatrice.

"I call this 'The Ghost Card Trick.'" His voice was deep, assuring, and melodious, consistent with his smooth handsome appearance. The stranger's social ease made Charlie nervous and suspicious. He had known other glib handsome men, but this one had an extra indefinable charisma that cut across ages and gender.

Joe Murphy sat next to the stranger. "Hey, Gefilte Fish! Check it out, man! This guy is a great magician!" He slapped the stranger's shoulder. "Show Charlie one of them tricks, pal!"

The stranger nodded and smiled at Charlie.

Charlie nodded back, then moved closer to the couch. Like everyone else in the room, he was drawn to the stranger. The man pulled a single card from the deck, the Joker. He folded the card vertically, but took care not to crease it. "This is the Ghost Card." He slapped it face down on the folding table, and put the rest of the deck in his safari jacket pocket. "Now, everyone, stare at the card and the psychic energy in this room will move it across and off the table. Just concentrate on the card. Nothing exists but the Ghost Card." He placed the palm of his hand several inches above the card. "Rise! Rise!" he said to the card. The room was silent. All eyes, including Charlie's, were on the card.

The crowd gasped as the card moved, then lifted to the palm of his hand.

"Now, fly!" the stranger commanded the card, moving his hand away from it. The card glided through the air, and across and then off the table. Everyone laughed and applauded, including Celia Fish. Charlie was glad to see his mother smile.

"Hot damn! How'd you do that, man?" shouted Joe Murphy.

The stranger chuckled, "Just an illusion. Actually I conned all of you. A very simple con. Magic is misdirection. While all of you were focused on the card, I moved my body ever so slightly like so." He tilted his body toward the couch.

"So what's that supposed to do?" asked Joe Murphy.

"Watch!" The handsome man slapped another card onto the table, bending it vertically as he did the Joker. "Now I'll move my body."

The card slid across the table. "Is this magic? No, it's not. Look what's next to me." He turned and pointed at the small air conditioner unit in the living room window. He cupped his hand over the cool breeze blowing from the unit's vent. "You've all been conned." He said this with a sparkling grin.

The room exploded into a roar of laughter. The stranger had captivated everyone. He stood up and approached Charlie, his hand extended for a shake. "Charlie, I was a friend of your dad's. He taught me that card trick and many others. He was a wizard with the cards, but you know that already."

He grabbed Charlie's hand and pumped it. His grip was firm, but not aggressive. "I'm Peter Abboud."

"Glad to meet you, Peter." The fact that his father never once mentioned this man made Charlie nervous.

"One of these days we have to sit down and reminisce about Morris. He used to talk about you all the time. He really loved you."

"Any time," Charlie said this with misgivings.

"How about breakfast tomorrow? Anywhere you want. It's on me." The stranger's words were more a challenge than an invitation.

"Lafayette Coney Island," said Charlie. His curiosity was stronger than his fears.

"My favorite place."

"My father's too," said Charlie.

••

the fourth day
of shiva

• 1976

ONLY THE HARDCORE customers ate breakfast at the Lafayette Coney Island at 7:00 A.M. Charlie Fish had been going here with his father since he was three. The greasy spoon dive had been a downtown Detroit institution since the Twenties, and it still hadn't lost its proletarian Depression-days veneer with its yellowing white tile walls, formica counters, and Greek-Syrian waiters with their white peaked caps, grimy aprons, sleeveless T-shirts, and beard-stubble faces. They barked orders at each other in Greek, Arabic, and pidgin-English. "One wid-out!" "Two wid onyuns only!" A short squat old man tended the grill. He was on display in the steam-coated front window, a spatula in one hand and tongs in the other, continuously turning the mound of loose gray hamburger meat with the spatula and flipping the line of hot dogs with the tongs.

Charlie Fish entered the Lafayette Coney Island. "Hey, Charlie!" Peter Abboud called out. He was sitting at the counter, dressed casually in a Led Zeppelin T-shirt and jeans.

Charlie was always fifteen minutes early. He was used to

waiting for people. Peter Abboud was the first to ever beat him to a rendezvous. He and Charlie shook hands.

"Good to see ya," said Peter with a warm smile. Charlie wasn't used to liking someone at first meeting. It took at least ten years to include someone on his short list of friends.

Charlie sat on the stool next to him. He wanted to trust Peter, but couldn't. He had seen the charm displayed at his mother's apartment and the violence at the cemetery.

The waiter walked over, a thin Syrian kid with a wisp of a mustache. "Whuh you gonna have?"

"I ordered two without, Charlie. What about you?"

"Same thing."

"Breakfast is on me. Next time you pay."

"Two widout!" the waiter shouted to the grill cook. The old man nodded, "Hokay." In one fluid movement, he placed a plate on the cutting board next to the grill, laid two hot dog buns on the plate, and opened them flat. He scooped loose meat onto each bun with a big metal spoon, drizzled brown chili onto each meat mound, then squeezed a stripe of yellow mustard onto the chili.

Charlie reached into his pants pocket and pulled out the plastic photo accordion that he had found in his father's wallet. He folded back the accordion to the picture of the small boy posed on Morris Fish's lap.

What's that?" Peter smiled, a slightly perplexed expression on his face.

"It's photos from my dad's wallet." He handed it to Peter. "Is that a picture of you?"

He stared at the photo. His face turned red, the first time that Charlie had seen him off-balance.

"Yes. It's me," he said quietly. "No wasting time with you, huh, Charlie? You get right to the point. Our father was like that, too."

Charlie blinked hard. He parroted Peter's words slowly inside his head . . . *our father*.

"Two widout for both of you!" the waiter barked as he placed the two plates of Coneys in front of Charlie and Peter. Under normal circumstances, this would be a scrumptious morning feast for Charlie, but breakfast was the last thing on his mind.

Peter turned to face him. He shrugged his shoulders and smiled helplessly. "Charlie, I was hoping that we'd get to know each other before I spilled the beans, but I guess that wasn't in the cards."

"Guess not." The photo shook in his hand.

"We don't choose our parents, Charlie."

"I know." His voice broke. He grabbed a napkin and quickly wiped his eyes before the tears could run.

• 1962 •

AT 6:30 P.M., dinner was over and Charlie sat in the living room of his parents' house waiting for The Mooch to show up.

The Mooch was a loudmouthed, almost completely hairless sixteen-year-old whose real name was Seymour Marcus.

sitting shiva

Nobody really liked him because he whined about everything and told meandering unfunny jokes, but he had a driver's license and a new Plymouth Barracuda. He was called "The Mooch" because every fifteen-year-old in the neighborhood could mooch rides off him. Passengers were required to laugh at the Mooch's jokes or they'd no longer be welcome in the Barracuda.

Charlie waited patiently. He really wanted to get away from his parents' house. They were still in the kitchen sniping at each other.

"This meat is like charcoal, Celia. I can't eat it."

"This isn't a restaurant. Besides, you like it raw and that just plain isn't healthy."

"And I suppose eating black charcoal is healthy, Celia? For Chrissakes, it's like eating dirt. Ribeye gotta be rare or it's got no taste!"

Charlie knew that the argument wasn't really about dinner. His parents had been fighting for the past three days. Charlie didn't want to know what it was really about. After dinner, they had kicked him out of the kitchen. This was unlike them because they always included him in their arguments. He either served as their arbitrator, deflector, or target. With the kitchen door closed, Charlie could hear only some of their words; mostly he could hear the sounds of their voices. His mother's sound was shrill and accusatory. His father's sound was a barking staccato.

"Where the fuck is he?" Charlie muttered to himself. The Mooch was a half-hour late. He was always late. He paced back and forth as he waited for his friends. He had told his parents that he was going to a party at Ellen Bronstein's house. Ellen was the school "brain." She hated Charlie and his goofball friends. The Mooch had promised to drive him, Metal Mouth Felch, and Joe Murphy to The Village of Love, one of Charlie's favorite places. The Village of Love was a downtown Detroit rock and roll joint named after a regional Detroit soul music hit single by Nathaniel Mayer. If it weren't for the folding chairs and makeshift stage, the Village would still look like the storage company warehouse that it once was. The Village of Love attracted a strange mix of people: high school punks like Charlie and his friends, street pimps and over-the-hill whores, weekend transvestites, and slumming middle-aged Grosse Pointer couples, along with a few Motown Records celebrities trying their best to be incognito.

For Charlie and his friends, the main attractions of The Village of Love were the watered-down booze that required no IDs and, above all, the music. Third-string Motown groups like the Contours, the Velvelettes, Junior Walker and the All-Stars, and Shorty Long would work out their stage acts at The Village. They'd electrify the crowds with synchronized movements, acrobatic splits, and soul-stirring vocals. To Charlie, these performers were unheralded geniuses.

The doorbell rang. Charlie breathed a sigh of relief. He opened the door. Instead of his friends, his Aunt Beatrice and Uncle Sheldon were on the porch. His uncle brushed past him without a word of greeting. His usually jovial bespectacled melon-shaped face quivered with rage. Aunt

Beatrice followed. Her eyes were bloodshot, her mascara smeared. "Where's your father, Charles?" she shouted at him, and rushed away before he could answer.

He felt panicky. Uncle Sheldon was a passive sweet man that told harmless Myron Cohen jokes with Yiddish punch lines. He was a half-head shorter than Aunt Beatrice, and quietly accepted her nagging and bullying. This was the first time that Charlie had seen his uncle take the lead.

Uncle Sheldon pushed open the kitchen door. Against Charlie's better judgement, he followed them into the kitchen.

"Morris, you sonofabitch!" Sheldon Sternbaum shouted. "This is the last goddamn time your sister and I clean up your crap!"

Morris's face flushed deep red. "What the hell are you talking about?"

"This woman! This piece of trash just came to my home this afternoon! To my home!"

"What? You gotta be crazy!" he stammered.

Celia's chin quivered.

Uncle Sheldon pressed both hands flat on the kitchen table and stared down at his brother-in-law. "Don't play stupid with me, you bastard! She scared the holy hell out of Beatrice while I was at work!"

"This animal introduced herself as your 'common-law wife.' She called me 'sister-in-law.' All that makeup like a clown! What is she, Morris, a goddamn Arab? She said her name is Abboud. She told me filthy things about orgies in motel rooms. Every graphic detail."

"What are all of you talking about?" sobbed Celia.

"Get out of my house!" Morris shouted. He started to get to his feet. Sheldon Sternbaum pushed him back into the chair. "Don't get out of that chair again, or so-help-me-God I'll beat the holy hell out of you, you sonofabitch!" His fists were clenched, his face pressed close to Morris Fish's face.

"My kid's here," Morris hissed under his breath.

Charlie froze in position as he watched the battle unfold.

"I think your son is old enough to know what kind of man his father is. Do you actually think that he doesn't know already?" shouted Sheldon Sternbaum.

"Everybody in town knows about you, except for Celia. She refuses to believe that you're no goddamn good!" screamed Aunt Beatrice.

"No! I don't want to hear any of this!" Celia moaned and clamped her hands over her ears.

Beatrice walked over to her and pulled her hands away from her ears. "You need to hear this! Maybe you'll leave my no-good brother once and for all! Celia, she brought her little Arab bastard to my house! She wanted me to get child support money from you. She threatened to go to every member of the family until she's paid off!"

Celia shut her eyes and shook her head violently like a child having a tantrum.

"I had to call the police to get her out of my house, Celia. Sheldon wasn't home! She was like a wild animal! A *vilda chaya!*"

"Goddamn you, Bea! Shut up!" Morris scrambled out of his chair.

"Sit down, you!" screamed Sheldon. He pushed his brother-in-law as hard as he could. Morris crashed down onto the
kitchen's linoleum-covered floor, smashing the back of his
head. He groaned and grabbed his head. Celia screamed.
Charlie was terrified. He couldn't move.

Beatrice bent down and pressed her face close to Celia's.
"Antoinette Abboud. That's her name, Celia. She's filth."
Tears ran down her face.

Celia clamped her hands back onto her ears. "I don't
want to hear this! No. No. No. No. No. No. No. No!"

"Stop it! Stop it, all of you! Stop! Leave my mother
alone!" Charlie's voice broke in a high-pitched bird-like
screech. He couldn't believe that this sound came out of
him. It scared him and everyone else in the kitchen.

"Let's go, Sheldon," Beatrice Sternbaum whimpered.
"Celia, he's my brother and I love him, but do yourself a favor
and divorce him."

Sheldon Sternbaum was so upset he was choking for air.
He pointed a fat index finger at Morris, but words couldn't
come out of his mouth.

He turned to Charlie. "I'm sorry, kid. I've never . . ." His
voice broke. He couldn't finish the sentence. He shook his
head in disgust and exited.

Beatrice glared at her brother, burst into tears, and ran
out of the kitchen.

Charlie could hear the front door slam shut as his aunt
left the house. The finality of this sound triggered a reaction
in Celia Fish. She began to sob; not the fake sobbing that
she used to get her own way. It was a wail of deep anguish.

"Mother, no," Charlie approached her. He was crying, too.

His father backed toward the kitchen door. "Goddamn liars. I'm through with the both of 'em. An' if you don't believe me, Celia, I'm packin' my bags and the hell with you," he muttered.

Celia Fish gripped the arms of her wheelchair and raised her body to a standing position. She stared at her husband. Her voice was a rasping whisper. "I hate you!"

He flinched as if he were slapped. He huffed and puffed with building rage. "Goddamn you! You take the word of my lying sister and her spineless husband over me?"

"You're the liar," she spat these words at him, clenching both fists and shaking them at him for emphasis.

He moved toward her in a boxer stance. "What did you call me, you goddamn miserable bitch?!"

She sat back down in the wheelchair. "Go to your other family, Morris." Her voice was tiny, quiet, steady. No histrionics. Charlie knew that she was serious.

"I'll shut your goddamn mouth permanently!" He smacked his right fist loudly against his left palm.

"If you're gonna hit somebody, hit me!" Charlie wedged his body between his parents.

A sadistic smile formed on his father's face. "Ooh. All of a sudden the little chicken is a tough guy." He slapped Charlie across the face. Charlie almost passed out. Blood flowed from his nose. He stumbled back, almost falling onto his mother in her wheelchair.

"Don't touch him or I'll call the police!" his mother screamed.

Morris's face flushed deep red. "I'll touch *you*, bitch!"

Charlie staggered, then wedged his body tighter between his parents. "You motherfucker. You dirty liar, if you ever touch my mother, I'll kill you!" Charlie screamed and pushed his father in the chest as hard as he could, sending him crashing back into the refrigerator. "Go to your slut! Nobody wants you here! I don't want you here!" Charlie trembled with rage and fear. He had never felt such anger.

His father grabbed the front of his shirt with both beefy hands. "You talk to *me* — your father — like that?" He pushed Charlie against the wheelchair. It rolled back, smashing into the wall. His mother shrieked.

"C'mon, chicken, hit me!" screamed his father.

Charlie clenched his fists.

"C'mon, little girl!"

Charlie glared at his father, unclenched his fists and dropped them to his sides. "No. Hitting is your answer to everything. I'm not like you. I'll never be like you."

"You're damn right. You're not like me. You're a weak little girl."

"Yes, you're right. I am a weak little girl. . . . If you're gonna beat the shit out of me, do it!"

"Why, you goddamn smartmouth punk!"

A car horn blasted from outside, stopping Morris Fish from hitting his son with a closed fist. The honking was persistent, bringing Morris back to reality. He lowered his fist. Tears filled his eyes. He let go of Charlie, and reeled several steps back. "Oh my God," he groaned. He displayed the palms of both hands in a gesture of surrender, and backed out of the kitchen.

Charlie heard the Mooch's blasting car horn again. He heard the sound of the front door flinging open, and his father leaving the house.

He bent down to his mother. "Are you all right?"

"Yes," she whispered. "Who's honking out there?"

"It's my friends. I'll tell them to leave."

"No, you go out with your friends. I don't want them to think that there's something wrong. It's nobody's business what goes on in this house."

"I don't want you to be alone."

"I'll call your Aunt Beatrice. She'll come over. I'll be okay. Don't worry about me. Go have a good time."

"No."

"I said, go!" Her words were strong, definite, final.

Charlie sighed heavily, and wiped the mucus and tears on his shirtsleeve. "Okay," he muttered. He tucked his shirt into his pants. He bent down and kissed his mother's cheek, steeled himself and left the house.

The Plymouth Barracuda was parked in the driveway behind the family Oldsmobile. As Charlie came out of his house, the sound of the Mooch's car horn hit his head like a sock full of nickels.

"Jeez Chrise! Whut kep' you, Fish?" Spittle flew out of the Mooch's Bazooka bubblegum-stuffed mouth.

Metal Mouth Felch and Joe Murphy were hooting and hollering from the backseat. They were drunk. "We got chicks meetin' us at the Village. Hot greaser chicks from Ferndale, Gefilte Fish! Picked 'em up at the Totem Pole!" shouted Joe Murphy.

"Pussy!" shouted Metal Mouth. He was already looped.

"Yeah! Blonde *shiksas*! Real blowjob queens! I told 'em we was polacks!" giggled the Mooch.

"Speak for yourself, Mooch! I'm a mick and proud of it!" said Joe Murphy.

"An' we got Night Train!" Metal Mouth waved a half-empty bottle of cheapo wine.

"Jeez Chrise! You wanna get me arrested?" whined the Mooch. "You know this is my old man's car!"

Every step toward the Barracuda was painful to Charlie. He smiled and tried to hide his anguish. Joe Murphy would understand. Metal Mouth Felch had his own screwy family to deal with. The Mooch would turn it into one of his bad jokes.

Joe flung open the back door. "C'mon, man!" Charlie climbed inside and grabbed the bottle of Night Train out of Metal Mouth's hand.

The Barracuda squealed out of the driveway and laid rubber on Westridge Avenue.

The Mooch liked to show off the horsepower of the muscle car. "The Highway Patrol got Barracuda engines an' nobody screws with the Highway Patrol," he'd brag.

Charlie guzzled the sickeningly sweet syrupy rotgut wine. The alcohol burned a beeline straight to his gut. Anything to kill his pain.

"Holy shit! Slow down! You tryin' to kill yourself, man?" laughed Joe Murphy. Charlie took another big swig.

"Jeez Chrise, Fish! Save some of that wine for us! We

went to Eight Mile and Wyoming an' paid a *shvoogie* five bucks for that shit!" whined the Mooch.

Charlie felt the near-hundred-proof booze head toward his stomach, then reverse its course. Barf surged out of his mouth and splattered onto the back of the glove-leather driver's seat.

"Aw, fuck!" screamed the Mooch. "You asshole! My old man's car!" The Barracuda jerked to a stop. "Get the fuck outta my car! You're never comin' in my car again, Fish!" He reached over and flung open the rear door. "Get out!"

Charlie staggered out of the car. Metal Mouth Felch stayed in the backseat of the Mooch's car. He was too drunk to do anything but point and laugh. The Mooch cursed and wiped up barf with the chamois cloth that he used for polishing the Barracuda.

Charlie began to cry. He ran down Granzon. Joe Murphy ran after him. Charlie tripped over his own feet, landing hard on his elbows and knees. Joe caught up with him. "Are you okay, Fish?" He helped him to his feet. "What's wrong, man?"

"My parents," he sobbed and sobbed and couldn't stop. "Sorry. S-sorry, Joe. I don't want to be a crybaby."

"Don't be ashamed. I cry too. One day I'll tell you about my old man and his good buddy Johnny Walker. C'mon. Let's walk and talk. We'll go to the Village another night. Those Ferndale girls were scags anyways."

Charlie and Joe walked slowly down Granzon toward their old hangout, the soon-to-be-demolished one-room schoolhouse on the junior high playground.

"I . . . I can't go home." These were the only words that Charlie could speak.

"You don't have to go home."

∵

JOE and Charlie sat on the top of a jungle gym on the junior high playground like they were kids again.

"You can hide out at my place as long as you want, Gefilte Fish."

"What about your parents?"

"Forget them. You'll stay in the cellar. Nobody goes there."

For a half-hour straight, Charlie talked and cried, and Joe listened.

When it turned dark, they took back alleys to the Murphy house and hopped the backyard fence. They quietly entered the house and crept down the stairs to the basement.

The cellar was tiny and cold, with one bare dangling lightbulb and floor-to-ceiling shelves filled with canned goods and jars of homemade preserves. Joe unrolled an old sleeping bag that his dad used for hunting Up North and laid it on the cellar's cement floor. For food, he brought down three hastily prepared peanut butter and jelly sandwiches and a quart of buttermilk. "If your folks come looking for you, Fish, I'm deaf an' dumb."

"Thanks, Joe."

"Forget it. Just pay me back the next time my old man

decides to punch the shit out of me." Joe put a bicycle lock on the cellar door, and said "goodnight" to Charlie.

Charlie tried to sleep. The cellar floor was too cold. Every time he'd close his eyes he'd see and hear the angry sounds and faces of his parents, and his aunt and uncle.

At 3:30 A.M. he heard the bicycle lock snap open. The cellar light flicked on. Morris Fish and Joe Murphys Senior and Junior stood in the doorway. Joe Sr. held tight to the scruff of his son's neck and shook him. A large red bruise covered the right side of Joe's face. Morris Fish's expression was a mix of worry and sadness. "Your mother is scared to death, do you know that?"

Without a word, Charlie pulled himself up from the cellar floor.

"I didn't tell him, Fish!" Joe called out.

"Shuddup, you!" Joe Sr barked, then cuffed his son's ear. "My kid's always been a damn liar, Morrie, but he can't fool me."

Charlie and his father left. On the ride home they didn't speak.

• 1976 •

CHARLIE COULDN'T GO back to his mother's apartment for the 10:00 A.M. Kaddish. He'd promised her, but he had too much to think about. He had lived his entire life as an only kid, and now he had a brother. Their Lafayette Coney Island breakfast was brief and cordial. They both knew that the tougher questions would have to be discussed in more private surroundings. Peter chose the occasion. He invited Charlie to dinner at his house in Dearborn for the following evening. Charlie accepted. Peter wanted him to meet his wife, Georgia, and his two daughters, Camille and Rozelle. Peter Abboud had the family and the house in the suburbs, the American dream. Charlie had a divorce, no kids, and a fleabag Detroit apartment. He questioned the true value of his own life.

He drove past all his old haunts. Even as a teenager, Charlie would drive past his old haunts whenever he needed to think, or escape, or both. He drove past the University of Detroit, where he went to architecture school, where he was mesmerized along with hundreds of other students as eighty-year-old R. Buckminster Fuller expounded for hours about futurism, architecture, and the universe. He drove past his old seedy student apartment on Tuller, where thousands of roaches would carpet the kitchen walls on rainy days. He drove past his former Oak Park home on Westridge. The Wangs, who owned the neighborhood Chinese restaurant, now lived in his house. The "F" for Fish was still on the screen door. He drove past Judy Weinstein's old house, beautiful Judy Weinstein. He had heard that she was married to David Rothman. He still hated Rothman, probably more than ever. He drove down Woodward Avenue, the Detroit metropolitan area's main drag. He passed the Totem Pole Drive-In in Royal Oak, the old rendezvous point for drag races and party location information. The "Three Bs" used to call it "The Toilet Bowl." They'd cruise for girls, and they'd "ratpack" and "moon" other cars. Every night in high school, they'd do the fifteen-mile Woodward loop from the Toilet Bowl in Royal Oak to Ted's Drive-In in Pontiac and back again. Charlie did "the loop" several times as he thought about his life, his father, and Peter Abboud.

He wondered what Peter Abboud was really like under the suave facade. Did he have Morris Fish's weaknesses of the flesh? Was he a psycho like his mother, Antoinette Abboud? He wondered if Peter had even the slightest resentment and jealousy toward him, if he picked up any of his mother's hatred toward Celia Fish, or if he hated Morris Fish for being an absentee father, present for an hour or a day at a time.

Charlie had his father's last name. Peter was born in the Fifties out of wedlock, and had to carry the stigma of being a "bastard." He grew up in hardscrabble Highland Park instead of safe suburban Oak Park.

Charlie pulled his car into the parking lot of Royal Oak's Shrine of the Little Flower. He shut off the engine and stared at the three-story-high stone Jesus Christ.

He wondered if Peter Abboud had killed his father.

•••

CHARLIE had had enough of the old memories, the nagging questions, and enough of the Detroit metropolitan area. He wound up on an expressway heading straight to Ypsilanti and Joe Murphy's house. Joe was the only one he could talk to.

He passed the expressway landmarks: the world's largest

tire, Detroit Metropolitan Airport, and the huge Ford Ypsi plant, where most of the city's population worked. He took the Michigan Avenue off-ramp. He drove along Michigan Avenue through Ypsilanti's central business district, a 1920s small-town time-warp lined with low-rise five-and-dime stores, pawnshops, diners, haberdasheries, and a barn-like drive-through liquor store. Only the revving and racing of oily-haired duck-tailed teenagers in big-tire high-riding hot rods punctured the quiet civility of Michigan Avenue. Hoods always made Charlie nervous, even though it was over ten years since high school.

He turned down Cross Street. Eastern Michigan University's most famous landmark, the phallus-shaped water tower, best known as "Big Dick," was in full view. Charlie went to EMU for his freshman year. Back then, there were only eight thousand students, seventy percent female, and he still couldn't get laid. He hated Ypsi. It was only five miles away from the idyllic intellectual hippie haven, Ann Arbor. Ypsi's housing costs were half those of Ann Arbor, so Joe Murphy had no complaints. He lived on a quiet tree-lined cul-de-sac. The two-story frame house had a front sitting porch and five bedrooms—large enough for Joe, his wife Lucy, and their three daughters.

Joe's old van, a former Wonder Bread truck, was parked in the driveway. Lucy's nondescript gray Plymouth, a former police car, was in front of the house. Lucy worked in the Michigan Public Defender's office, so she was privy to police surplus auctions. Charlie parked behind Joe's van.

Lucy was Joe Murphy's opposite: Sicilian, beautiful, and intensely opinionated against Joe's laid-back Irish good nature, whacked-out sense of humor, and battered wrestler's face. On the surface, their marriage was a mass of contradictions, but they were a solid match.

Before Charlie reached the front porch, Joe opened the door. "Gefilte Fish!" he bellowed. He was only wearing a pair of baggy swim trunks. Muscles and blue veins bulged on every inch of his body. Joe Murphy was his best buddy, but Charlie hated the sight of his body, especially the blue veins. His guts turned, as Joe grabbed him in a bearhug and squeezed the breath out of him. He pulled him inside the house and shut the door. "Perfect timing, man. The Jacuzzi is bubbling. Darla got some Thai stick, and I got a case of Upper Canada in the fridge."

"I don't know if I want to get high," stammered Charlie. Super-strong dope usually exaggerated whatever emotion he was feeling, especially paranoia.

"Why stand on ceremony after all these years, Charlie Fish?" Darla called out. She was sitting on the living room couch, sucking on a toothpick-thin Thai stick joint. She wore a baby blue old lady-style bathing suit with ruffles that might have been bought at a local Salvation Army Thrift Shop. Her once perfect Betty Grable ice-cream-blonde legs had become blobs of cellulite.

"Hi, Darla." Charlie smiled at his old friend and lover with mixed feelings of pity, revulsion, love, and a touch of horniness.

He walked to the couch, bent down, and kissed her cheek. "It's always good to see your friendly face."

"I like your friendly face too," she giggled, wrapped her arms around the back of his neck and kissed him back; a long desperate kiss on the mouth. She smelled like hospital antiseptic. Charlie pulled away from her as gently as possible. An expression of hurt registered briefly on her face, then her playful friendly smile returned. Before he could apologize, Joe grabbed his arm. "C'mon, man. Take a load off. You haven't seen the hot tub yet."

"But I don't have a swim suit."

"So what? Strip down to your rusty undies. I've seen 'em before, man."

"So have I." Darla giggled. "Take it off. Take it all off."

"What about Lucy and the kids?"

"Shit. They're all at gymnastics practice. Fucking gymnastics is gonna break me. You wouldn't believe what a pair of goddamn gymnastics shoes cost. All three of them kids gotta have goddamn gymnastics shoes. Remember when we were kids? We wore Keds and liked it. C'mon, Charlie, drop trou'!"

Charlie shrugged his shoulders, blushed, and dropped his pants, revealing Fruit of the Looms that hadn't been changed since the day of his father's funeral.

"Nice legs." Joe whistled and guffawed.

"I think they're cute," Darla teased.

Charlie followed Joe through the house. Darla lagged behind. To Charlie, the Twenties-vintage craftsman house was a knockout, especially the parquet floor that spread into every room on the first floor. This was the house's most stunning feature. The second floor was a dormer added in the Fifties.

They walked through the screened-in back porch and entered the back yard. A ten-foot-high wooden fence surrounded the small yard, allowing maximum privacy from snoopy neighbors. The California redwood hot tub was large enough to comfortably seat four adults. A beer cooler was conveniently located next to the tub. Joe opened the cooler. It was filled with longneck bottles of Canadian beer. Joe grabbed three bottles and handed one to Charlie and one to his sister. "Fuck the world!" he shouted with a giant grin, as he lowered his massive body into the water. "Don't just stand there like a mongoloid, Fish!" He popped off the bottle-cap in his teeth for emphasis.

Charlie laughed at Joe's antics, then lowered his body into the bubbling water. He hadn't laughed in almost a week. Joe Murphy always knew how to take Charlie's mind off the worst moments in his life.

• **1962** •

CHARLIE FAKED A "twenty-four-hour flu" to stay home from school. His mother had bought the lie because he'd spent the previous night on the Murphys' cold cellar floor.

Luckily for him, she was out of the house. She was at Stouffer's eating lunch with Aunt Beatrice, who was probably trying hard to convince her to divorce his dad.

Morris Fish was at his card club, or at least that's where he'd said he was.

Charlie snuggled under the covers in his parents' bed, watching "Lunchtime With Soupy." He could use a good laugh. He watched Soupy Sales read "The Words of Wisdom" that were scrawled in white chalk on the blackboard: "Be true to your teeth and they won't be false to you." He tried to laugh as Soupy launched into his loping side-to-side, front-to-back "Soupy Shuffle," rotating his big polkadot bowtie like a plane propeller, while Pookie the Hippo sang "C-O-W Spells a Cow." His parents, along with many other Detroit parents, thought that Soupy Sales' corny jokes and cream pies were a bad influence on their children. Soupy could usually make Charlie laugh, but he wasn't laughing today.

The telephone rang on the nightstand next to the bed. Charlie picked it up. "Hello?"

"Hello, Charlie," the voice whispered. "Are you playing hooky today?"

A jolt of terror hit him. "Fuck you, bitch!" he screamed and slammed down the receiver. He grabbed the phone and yanked the cord out of the wall. He wanted to strangle his father with the chord.

"Son of a bitch, I'll fix you!" he screamed at his father, even though he wasn't there. Charlie scrambled out of the bed. He thought about hopping a bus and taking it as far as it would go, and never coming back to Oak Park. He thought about running to the bathroom and emptying all of his mother's many bottles of pills into his mouth. He thought about killing his father. He thought about killing that psycho bitch. Who was she? What hold did she have on his father?

Charlie realized that he didn't know his father at all. Was everything about him a lie? He'd find out and he'd tell his mother the truth no matter how much it hurt, even if he had to tear the house apart.

"You goddamn liar!" he shouted as he ran to his parents' dresser. He pulled out the bottom two drawers, and emptied them, grabbing pairs of his father's black thick-and-thin dress socks, his white Fruit of the Looms, and dry cleaner boxes containing his folded starched white shirts. He thought that if he could find the bitch's phone number, he'd call her and make his own phone death threats at three in the morning.

"I hate you!" he shouted and ran to the bedroom closet. He snatched his father's black mohair suits, Sansabelt slacks, and Italian knit shirt-jacs off wooden hangers and tossed them onto the bed. He pulled out every pocket, and only found lint, one crisp two-dollar bill, and a couple of monogrammed snotrags.

He grunted in frustration and ran to the kitchen. He opened the kitchen closet and grabbed a folding stepstool. He carried it into the hallway outside his parents' bedroom and set it directly under the attic hatch in the hall ceiling. He unfolded the stool to its maximum height, climbed to the top, and slid open the attic hatch. He pulled himself up into the attic. The dark space smelled of mothballs. He brushed cobwebs away from his face. Cardboard packing boxes and old suitcases crammed the attic. His parents' family heirlooms and other articles of sentimental value were kept there.

He opened every box. He found Depression-era dishes that had been given away at Detroit neighborhood movie theaters. He found glass figurines that his mother had collected from trips to Windsor, Ontario during her teenage years. He found family photo albums dating back to Czarist Russia. He found a stack of his father's World War Two overseas love letters, all tied together with a red ribbon. Charlie removed the ribbon. Letter after letter began with "Dear baby-doll" and ended with "I love you. Morris."

"More goddamn lies!" Charlie shouted as he threw the letters across the room.

In the rear of the attic was his father's metal Army trunk. He pulled open the lid. Morris Fish's olive green dress uniform was folded in a square. The two bronze stars, a Purple Heart, and several bar decorations were pinned to the jacket. Charlie unfolded the jacket and pants. He pulled out the pockets. They were empty. A pair of spit-shined Army dress shoes and a dress hat were on the bottom of the trunk. He slipped his hand inside each shoe and only found a metal shoehorn. He grabbed the dress hat. He yanked out a strip of cardboard and the onionskin paper lining that kept the hat's shape intact. An envelope fell out of the hat. A 1960 postmark was on it. The envelope was addressed to "Morris Fish c/o The Produce Club." He opened the envelope. There was no letter inside, only a black-and-white Polaroid snapshot. He stared at the photo. A woman in her thirties posed lasciviously. She had huge flabby breasts with silver-dollar-sized dark nipples and a mane of ratted-up black hair. Her eyes scared him. They were the ravenous eyes of a beast surrounded by raccoon-like rings of mascara. Charlie turned over the photo. On the back was an inscription in florid purple-ink handwriting: "You'll always be my big strong man. Antoinette."

He couldn't stop staring at the photo. He had seen women like her on Amateur Night at the Stone Burlesk— mean over-the-hill barflies down on their luck shaking their moneymakers, cursing and spitting at the taunting audience. Could his father really love her?

Charlie ripped up the photo and threw the scraps on the attic floor. He started to tear the envelope, but stopped. The return address was written on the back flap: Third Street in Highland Park. He knew the neighborhood. It was near the Michigan State Fairgrounds. Charlie went there twice a year to eat corndogs and cotton candy, and gape at thousand-pound hogs and sideshow freaks like the Alligator Boy and the Hermaphrodite.

He folded the envelope in half and tucked it inside his pants pocket. He climbed out of the attic, put on a pair of shoes, and left the house.

He walked the mile to Oak Park High School. It was one in the afternoon, second period lunch hour. Joe Murphy would be out in the school parking lot cadging a Camel with the hoods leaving on the "Greenberg Express." Every day at second period lunch hour, Roy Greenberg's Corvair would pick up school-skipping seniors, hoods, and other malcontents for an afternoon of poker and beer drinking in his parents' garage, or an exclusion to a downtown Detroit poolhall,

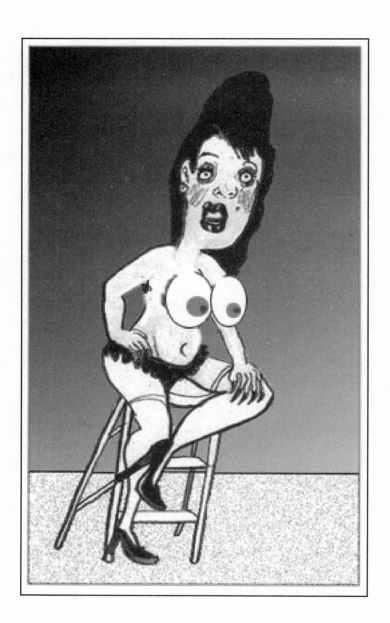

or, if they were very lucky, a gang-bang with Bridget, a forty-year-old "nympho" waitress at Gondola's Pizzeria. On some afternoons, Joe Murphy would board the Greenberg Express. On others, he'd only bum cigarettes, hang out, and swap dirty jokes with the hoods.

"Hey, Frankenstein!" Charlie Fish shouted as he walked through the parking lot, past the teachers' Fords and Chevys, past the Preps' Vettes and Daddy's Caddies, and past the hoods' chopped-and-channeled, primer-coated, twenty-year-old hot rods. Joe Murphy, Roy Greenberg, five other teenaged boys, and Rita Fuchs—better known as "Rita Fucks"—hovered around the Corvair. They were furtively passing a paper bag containing a bottle of Sloe Gin.

Joe Murphy waved at Charlie and tried to grin, but half of his mouth was swollen and black and blue, as were both eyes.

"Jesus Christ, Joe! Did your old man do that?"

Joe shrugged his shoulders helplessly. "No big thing, man. I'm a hard head. I don't feel no pain. One of these days I'll put that drunk sonofabitch out of his misery. How's by you? Did the shit hit the fan at the old homestead?"

"My old lady can't look at me without turning on the waterworks, and my old man won't talk to me. Can you believe that? He fucks up and then he blames me. Take a look at what I found." He pulled the envelope out of his pocket. "I got that psycho cunt's address."

Joe dropped his big hand on Charlie's shoulder. "Whatever you wanna do, Charlie, I'm on your side."

∙∙

CHARLIE and Joe got off the Woodward bus right across the street from the Michigan State Fairgrounds's landmark attraction, the world's largest stove, a three-story-high seventy-five-year-old rusting relic relocated from the St. Louis Exposition.

"Third Street is about four blocks off Woodward," said Charlie as they turned down Piggins. Dutch Elm Disease had long taken its toll on this once lush tree-lined residential street. Apartment buildings and red brick duplexes that had been middle-class had degenerated into slums packed with large black, Lebanese, and hillbilly families.

"What are we gonna do, Charlie?"

"I dunno," he muttered and fingered the handle of the bread knife that was in his jacket pocket.

They turned left on Third. Although it was a busy one-way commuter artery, Third Street was very much a residential street like Piggins. Charlie slowed his pace. He stared at the addresses on the apartments and duplexes. "Her place is a block down on this side of the street. I don't want her to see us coming."

Charlie ran across Third. Joe followed. They ducked down a narrow walkway next to a brownstone. They ran past a pack of large and small mongrels in the brownstone's backyard. The half-starved vicious creatures snarled, yelped, and tried to lunge through the fence to get at Charlie and Joe.

They turned onto an alley, stepping carefully over and around overturned garbage cans, dead rats, car parts, and broken beer bottles that were strewn everywhere. Charlie stared into every yard, every abandoned garage, and down every driveway and walkway. He turned into a dark passage between two apartment buildings. Joe followed. The passage was so narrow they had to slide though it sideways. At the end of the passage, Charlie stopped. They could peer out at Third Street without being seen. "That's her place." Charlie pointed across the street at a shabby one-story frame house with metal security grills covering every window, except, incongruously, a large picture window. There were no drawn shades, drapes, or blinds to assure privacy. The living room, illuminated by a plaster Venus de Milo lamp, could be seen from the street by pedestrians and passing traffic. The walls and furniture were shades of green, like Celia Fish's living room. Charlie felt ill.

He could see a Raid bug spray commercial playing on the color TV set: cartoon roaches screaming with eyeballs and tongues protruding out of their heads. Charlie used to think that the commercial was funny because it reminded him of a Tex Avery cartoon, but now he felt like a sprayed roach. The Fish household didn't even have a color TV. He wondered if his father had paid for the color TV in Antoinette Abboud's living room. He cautiously emerged from the passage to get a closer look at the illuminated room.

"What are you doing, Fish?" Joe Murphy hissed.

"I don't see anybody in that living room."

"There's nobody home. I bet she does the same trick as my old lady. She turns on the TV set when she leaves the house, so the burglars will think somebody's there."

"I think she's there. I want to wait."

Joe Murphy groaned.

"You can always leave, Joe. I'm not keeping you here."

"As long as the cigarettes hold out, Fish, I'll hold out."

They squatted on their haunches in the narrow passage, smoked Joe's unfiltered Camel cigarettes, and waited.

.•.

THEY waited for several hours, watching rush hour traffic build and then thin out. A mound of cigarette butts formed at their feet. They had gone through almost two packs.

The light in Antoinette Abboud's living room flicked off. The frame house's front door opened.

"I knew she was home," said Charlie.

A large overweight woman in her forties stepped out and onto the front porch. Only the huge ratted-up mane of black hair identified her as the same woman in the photo that Charlie found.

"That's her. That's her," said Charlie.

Antoinette Abboud triple-locked the door, looked in all directions for safety's sake, and stepped off the porch and onto the sidewalk. She wore a too-tight scarlet red dress that showed off every roll of fat. The color of her lipstick matched the color of her dress.

"Whoo boy. She's an ergly one. A goddamn skank," groaned Joe Murphy. "Your old man either needs some glasses or a headshrinker."

Charlie didn't answer. He couldn't stop staring at her. He felt like running across Third Street and beating her until her face was bloody, until it matched her dress and her lipstick. He felt like dashing headlong into Third Street rush hour traffic, and letting the cars smash him into a bloody mess.

Antoinette Abboud walked to the padlocked driveway double-gate next to the house. She unlocked the gates and pulled them open. A recently Simonized lime-green Cadillac Biarritz with a matching leather Landau hardtop was parked in the driveway. Its sharp right-angle fins pointed skyward. She opened the driver door and slid her bulk inside.

"What do you wanna do, Charlie?"

"Nothing. Not today."

"Cripes. We came all the way out here for nothing?"

"I just wanted to see her."

· 1976 ·

JOE, CHARLIE, AND Lucy leaned back at the dining room table, after a couple of fat Jamaican spliffs, three liters of California wine, and a delicious dinner of venison steaks and morel mushrooms sautéed in burgundy, courtesy of one of Joe Murphy's Up North hunting trips and Lucy's culinary skills. With the Murphys' three kids staying at a neighbor's house, they were ready for a night out in nearby Ann Arbor. Blues guitar legend Freddie King was playing at the Blind Pig, a former downtown "A-Square" gutbucket that was slowly being gentrified into a fern bar by its suburban Detroit owners.

"What's keeping Darla?" grumbled Lucy Murphy. She was always the person in charge of coordinating social events. Somebody has to do it, she'd always say.

"Who the fuck knows. She's been in that john forever," said Joe.

"God, she's always doing this. We'll be late, and we'll wind up with crummy seats." Lucy fumed.

"I'll get her," said Charlie.

He walked upstairs to Joe and Lucy's bathroom. He knocked on the closed bathroom door. "Darla. It's Charlie." His voice was gentle. "We gotta go."

There was no response. He knocked again. "Are you all right?"

"Yes," she said weakly, "I'm okay. I'm just not going."

"Why?"

"I look like crap."

"C'mon, Darla. You know I don't care about that. Besides, I look like crap too."

She didn't answer. He could hear quiet sobs.

"Darla, you're my friend. We've been friends for years. We'll go out tonight. Hear some kick-ass blues."

"No."

"Look, we don't have to go to the Blind Pig. I'll take you somewhere nice. Just you and me. It'll be a date. We'll go to the Ann Arbor Hilton bar."

There was no response, not even sobbing.

As Charlie sighed and headed toward the stairs, the bathroom door opened. Darla came out. He turned and smiled at her. She was dressed in an outdated blue pastel pants suit that was probably once one of Lucy Murphy's old maternity outfits.

"Let's go to the Hilton," she smiled sheepishly at Charlie.

"You look great, Darla," he lied.

∴

CHARLIE and Darla entered the Ann Arbor Hilton bar, a sport-jacket-and-tie joint for U of M faculty members, visiting U of M parents, and local Ann Arbor businessmen. This wasn't the Blind Pig or Mr. Flood's Party crowd. Charlie and Darla's attire didn't fit.

The hostess approached. Like the bartenders and waitresses, she was a college student. Although she had the primly attractive look of a WASP sorority president, she smiled pleasantly at Charlie and Darla, and led them to a table in the darkest remotest booth in the room.

The indirect lighting and cozy booths were tailor-made for wife-swappers and wife-cheaters. Quiet Cal Tjader jazz was tastefully piped in as background music.

Charlie and Darla slid into the booth. She sat so close to him she was almost in his lap. "Great place," she said, then lit a Kool cigarette.

Charlie felt his pocket to make sure that he didn't leave his wallet at Joe's house. An evening at the Ann Arbor Hilton bar would be expensive. At the Blind Pig, he'd be able to order one bottle of Stroh's and nurse it for the entire evening. He'd much rather be listening to the blues, but Darla had become like a big sister to him and she was hurting.

He could only barely converse with her. The medication had taken its toll on her once-sharp mind. She babbled endlessly, using words like "livid" and phrases like "you really know how to hurt a guy" over and over. She laughed in all the wrong places at his jokes. He felt ashamed that his own mind was drifting away from her conversation. He thought about his dead father, his mother, Antoinette Abboud, and Peter Abboud. He felt guilty about staying away from his mother's "house of shiva" for an entire day.

The waitress came to the table. She was a pretty redhead with soft pink skin, probably a Tri Delt from Grosse Pointe Farms. She smiled at Charlie. "Can I get you something?"

He inhaled sharply. He liked her looks.

Darla had no problem placing an order. "I'll have a Mai Tai."

Oh shit, thought Charlie, an expensive girlie drink with a bamboo umbrella.

"I'll have . . . uh . . . a Tuborg," he said. If he had ordered a Stroh's instead of an imported beer, he would've wound up looking like a cheapskate or an unsophisticated bumpkin to this lovely young waitress. He made eye contact with her. She blushed. What he liked most about redheads was that their fair skin betrayed them and made it impossible to hide their emotions. The physical attraction was obvious on both ends.

"Thank you," she smiled again, then walked slowly away from the table, giving Charlie a clear view of her lovely tight little ass.

"She's pretty, isn't she?" said Darla.

"Oh, I didn't notice," Charlie lied and wished that he had ordered a double shot of Bushmill's to go with the beer. He felt bad that he had flirted with the waitress, a stranger, while on a "date" with Darla, his friend. He wondered how he'd be able to get the waitress's name and phone number without Darla knowing it. "Have you seen Toddy lately?" he asked her.

"He lives with his father and wants to be called 'Todd' now. He's over six feet tall. Can you believe it? . . . The last time I called him 'Toddy' he bit my head off. He was livid. I told him 'Toddy, you really know how to hurt a guy.'"

Darla was starting to get on his nerves. He decided that he'd get her plastered on mixed drinks. She'd pass out and he'd be able to freely talk to the waitress. He had only one credit card in his wallet, and he only used it for emergencies. For Charlie, getting the redhead's name and phone number qualified as an emergency. Two hours passed. Charlie and Darla consumed beers and Mai Tais. Unfortunately the cocktails only barely affected her and, if possible, made her even *more* talkative and alert. Charlie was the one who was getting groggy from the beers. He knew that the bill had pushed past twenty bucks and that his devious plan was only contributing to his further impoverishment. Serves me right for being an insensitive prick, he thought.

Charlie waved the waitress over. She smiled and strolled to the table, gently rolling her soft hips for his benefit. He handed her the credit card. He could hardly hide the expression of disappointment on his face. As she took his card, the tips of her fingers lightly brushed his hand. "Would you like a receipt?" she asked with a lilt in her voice.

"Yes," he answered, without even knowing why he'd need a receipt since his paltry income from the city of Detroit's Department of Urban Planning hardly warranted any tax deductions.

The waitress returned with Charlie's Master Charge card, the charge slip, a ballpoint pen, and the receipt on a little plastic tray. Charlie filled out the slip with the pen and gave it to the redhead. She smiled when she saw the fifteen percent tip, and gave Charlie back the carbon copy. "Have a nice evening and drive safe," she said to both of them, but looking straight at Charlie. He sighed and pocketed the credit card and the carbon copy. She walked away, giving him another ass shot.

As Darla slid out of the booth, Charlie peeked at the receipt. On the back was a salution, printed meticulously in blue ballpoint ink: "Thank you. Bonnie."

Charlie smiled and repeated the name "Bonnie" inside his head. He slipped the receipt inside his shirt pocket.

As he left the Ann Arbor Hilton bar with Darla, Charlie tried not to glance in the direction of the lovely redhead.

The next time he was in Ann Arbor, he'd call the bar and ask for Bonnie.

∴

CHARLIE could never handle alcohol, even beer. At 2:30 A.M., he was sound asleep on the fold-out couch-bed in the Murphys' living room. An army blanket was in a balled-up heap next to him. He was folded in a jackknife position on the mattress. He wore only a pair of jockey shorts.

Darla Murphy tiptoed down the stairs and into the living room. She was completely nude. She walked to the couch and stared at Charlie. With one quick movement, she grabbed the blanket, draped it over Charlie, and scooted underneath. She pressed her body tight against him. Upon feeling her soft cool skin squeezing against his bare back, he jolted awake. His dick stiffened immediately. "Warm me up, Charlie. I'm cold," she cooed into his ear.

"Jesus Christ, Darla." He sat upright.

"Surprise. Surprise," she giggled, slid her hand inside his undies, and lightly stroked his stiff penis. "Ooh. You must be glad to see me."

"No, Darla. Please." He removed her hand firmly but gently, and turned to face her.

"You know you want it, Charlie." She squeezed her body close. They were belly-to-belly. "Soft warm pussy," she whispered into his ear.

He stared into her eyes. They were dull junkie eyes. He felt no real emotional contact with her as he had only a few years before. She baby-kissed a path from his mouth to his neck to his chest to his belly. He felt her take his penis into her mouth. He shut his eyes and felt her warm wet tongue encircling his dick. He enjoyed the sensation. If it were anyone other than Darla, his friend, he'd fuck her and deal with the consequences later. His feelings of pleasure turned to nausea, then shame, and then anger. He pushed her head away from his cock. "No! Darla, no! Goddamn it!" he said this louder than he intended.

Her eyes filled with tears. She looked like a child that had been slapped. "You used to love me," she sobbed.

"I still do."

"You have a funny way of showing it."

"I don't love you *that way*. Not anymore."

"It's the way I look, isn't it? I'm just a big fat slob," she cried bitterly.

"No. It's not you. I'm just not ready for anything serious." He tilted her chin up and stared directly into her eyes. "Listen to me." This time he felt emotional contact. "I've got a dead marriage, a dead old man, and a goddamn half-brother that just crawled out of the woodwork. I don't know my asshole from my elbow right now. Other than anger, I got no emotions left. I got nothing to give anyone. Can you understand that, Darla?"

"I'm sorry, Charlie," she whispered. "I was being selfish."

"No, you weren't. I'm the one that's selfish right now."

"Our timing has always been shitty, hasn't it, Charlie?" She smiled weakly.

"Absolutely."

"Maybe one day it won't be shitty." She smiled hopefully.

"Maybe," he lied. Charlie knew that she'd never escape the medication.

"Can I stay here for the rest of the night, Charlie? We'll just cuddle. Okay?"

"Okay," he said reluctantly.

He folded back into a jackknife position and shut his eyes. She snuggled spoonlike behind him, her soft flesh against his back, ass, and legs. She closed her eyes. They were cozy.

•••

the fifth day
of shiva

· 1976 ·

CHARLIE ARRIVED AT his mother's apartment complex near 1:00 P.M. Although it was the fifth day of shiva, there were no parking spaces within a two-block radius of the apartment building. He figured that it was near lunchtime and the free platters of bagels and lox had probably arrived and so did "the moochers." He cursed as he squeezed the Bumblebee between two trucks on Kipling. His head ached with a beer hangover. He wasn't used to chugging beers. Marijuana was his "high" of choice.

He walked down Kipling, muttering under his breath. He knew that he'd have to face all those people again. Deep down, he was jealous of his mother's social skills. She was well loved by friends, family, and passing acquaintances.

He always felt that his mother loved people and hated him. Their personal differences were too great. Throughout his life he had greatly disappointed her and she never let him forget it. He questioned too many conventions, made too many sick jokes, and wore his clothes too sloppily. She wanted him to be a clean-cut suburban Jewish man with a clean-cut suburban Jewish family, possessing only the unembellished amiable banter of news, weather, sports, and not much else. He felt that she had always reached out to acquaintances and strangers to avoid daily contact with him. Throughout most of his teenage years, she devoted her time to endless City of Hope Cancer Fighter meetings, dinner dances, and fundraisers. To Charlie, her preoccupation with charity and socializing was only slightly understandable as a reaction to the years that she spent in near-isolation in the Herman Kiefer Hospital TB ward. He had always tried to fully understand, but couldn't get past his own feelings of loneliness.

He walked the two blocks up Parklawn to the apartment building. He gritted his teeth, opened the front door, and entered. The living room was packed with people: neighbors, a couple of ancient Nosanchuk cousins that he only barely remembered, and strangers who looked like they might be Celia Fish's favorite bank teller, her favorite delicatessen waitress, or her favorite manicurist.

Charlie smiled and nodded and slid through the crowd of wellwishers. He could see his mother sitting on the couch and his ex-wife Nancee sitting next to her. Nancee's arm was draped sympathetically around his mother's shoulders. Charlie's heart jumped with surprise. Nancee hadn't talked to him since she walked out months ago. She was Celia's dream come true: a nice Jewish girl from a wealthy family. The divorce was one more disappointment for his mother. After two years of marriage, Nancee tired of the fleabag downtown Detroit apartment. She tired of the spaghetti and cheapo Cribari red wine dinners with Charlie's mixed bag of friends: the Wayne State grad students, the babbling dopers, and the working-class heroes. She tired of the endless discussions, the minutiae of Marxism versus anarchism, Wilhelm Reich versus Fritz Perls, Bucky Fuller versus Mies van der Rohe, and the ultimate quandary: Curly Howard versus Shemp Howard. She tired of the roaches and cigarette butts in the ashtrays. She tired of the secondhand furniture, the banging radiator, the groaning refrigerator, and the peeling wallpaper. She tired of looking in all directions whenever she'd leave the apartment or get out of her car. She was especially tired of waiting for Charlie to become Frank Lloyd Wright while living on his $112-a-week City of Detroit urban planning department salary and her $75-a-week inner-city Detroit teacher's aide salary. She longed for a kitchen without cockroaches. She longed for clean walls and carpets that weren't a patchwork of remnants.

Above all, she wanted children. Charlie didn't. He knew that he'd wind up trapped in the suburbs for the rest of his life.

Charlie bent down to kiss his mother's cheek. She turned her head away from him, a cold expression on her face. He always knew that the colder her fury the angrier she was. "I'm sorry that I wasn't here yesterday, mother. I needed a break. I was getting stir crazy here."

"I don't want anything to do with you," she said quietly, so only he could hear her words.

Charlie displayed his palms in a gesture of helplessness. "Okay, mother. Okay."

"Hi, Charlie." Nancee looked up at him with a sad apologetic smile. Her voice broke through his feelings of guilt. "I just heard about your dad yesterday."

"Hi, Nancee." He kissed her cheek. She smelled like cocoa butter. She still looked good to him, even though she had trimmed her Angela Davis-sized Jewish Afro to a manageable suburban pageboy and her Rubenesque figure had grown even rounder. He wondered if she was pregnant.

Charlie had known Nancee since high school.

• 1974 •

To psych up enough nerve to arrive alone at the ten-year Oak Park High School reunion, Charlie Fish ate two quaaludes, smoked six joints of Colombian, and downed two cans of Mickey's Big Mouth malt liquor. When he felt that his legs were sufficiently rubbery and that an I-don't-give-a-shit attitude was planted firmly in his mind, he climbed inside the Bumblebee and drove to the St. Regis Hotel, which was only a mile from his ratty apartment on Gladstone. Next door to the venerable Fisher Building and across the street from the Chrysler Building, the St. Regis was a fairly new hotel built to add a touch of class to Detroit's New Center area. It was an architect's attempt to recreate the look of a French chateau.

Charlie parked the Bumblebee in the Fisher Building lot and walked toward the St. Regis. He wore a blue jean jacket and blue jean pants with a moth-eaten Hawaiian shirt and a gaudy hand-painted Forties tie, both courtesy of the Salvation Army; this was his hippie version of formal attire.

Arriving cars lined up in the St. Regis Hotel's rotunda.

Men in dark suits and women in dress gowns emerged from the mostly late-model cars. Charlie began to feel intimidated. He thought about ducking down an alley and entering through a service door. He had heard that many of his classmates had become professionals, had married into money, and had gone into family businesses. The rest had wound up drifting or fucking up royally. Charlie fit into the fuck-up category. He knew that he'd probably be the only fuck-up to have the nerve to attend the reunion.

"Screw it," he said to himself and walked toward the rotunda. He really didn't care what the others thought about him. He just wanted to see Judy Weinstein. When he had last heard, she was at grad school in Ann Arbor. He had often thought about going up to Ann Arbor to see her, but he didn't know how she'd react. They were two very different people. She didn't get high. She wanted children and a house in the suburbs. She wanted a man with a career, and his city of Detroit mural-painting job would never qualify as a career. Although he felt deep down that he wasn't good enough for her, Charlie always held onto a tiny light of optimism. She was his junior high first love. He thought that she might have the same feelings toward him.

He entered the St. Regis lobby. The faux-French Chateau exterior motif carried into the lobby. Charlie looked around the room for a familiar face or a bulletin board indicating the reunion ballroom's location. "Charles Fish!" a too-perky female voice called out.

He turned behind him to see Ellen "the brain" Greenstein, the class valedictorian, student council vice-president, and captain of the debate team. Ellen Greenstein had always been cute in a chipper Julie Andrews way, but she and her honor roll friends had always ignored Charlie and the Three Bs, considering them to be malcontents and "greasers." They especially considered Howieschultz to be the ultimate traitor. He was a straight "A" student hanging out with "losers." Howieschultz considered the honor-roll bunch to be a pack of boring pseudo-intellectual snobs and brownnosers. He liked cruising for burgers, late-night card games, rock and roll, and easy "pussy." Being in Los Angeles, Howieschultz cited distance and business obligations as a legitimate excuse for not attending the reunion, even though he would've had sufficient bragging rights as a successful Hollywood attorney.

"Charles, you look lost. C'mon with me." Ellen looped her arm in his and steered Charlie down a corridor. "I've been here all day getting things ready. I'm on the reunion committee, so I know where everything is in this hotel."

"Thanks, Ellen." Charlie couldn't believe that Ellen "The Brain" Greenstein was actually speaking to him.

"So, what have you been doing with yourself for ten years, Charles? Judging from your outfit, you look like you've been tuning in, turning on, and dropping out," she chortled at her own weak attempt at humor.

"I'm an urban planner," he lied, or at least stretched the truth.

"Oh really? I'm impressed." Her eyebrows lifted with surprise.

"What about you, Ellen?"

"I'm at Brandeis."

"Good school."

"I teach there."

"Now I'm the one that's impressed."

"Well, I worked hard to get where I am. There are times, though, when I wished that I had more fun . . . like you, Charles." He knew that that this was more a subtle dig than a true conviction from Ellen "The Brain" Greenstein.

They arrived at the Lafayette Ballroom lobby. People milled around the lobby's no-host bar. The Ballroom's double doors were locked. She led Charlie to a card table in front of the doors. Stacks of alphabetically arranged nametags were on the table. Ellen found the tag with Charlie's name on it, and slapped the sticky side onto his jean jacket pocket. "There you go. Now everyone will know who you are under all that hair," she chortled.

An egg-shaped bespectacled couple walked up to the table. Charlie didn't recognize them. "Ellen Greenstein!" squealed the egg-shaped woman.

"Brenda Bidlofsky, is that you?" Ellen squealed back.

"Brenda Bidlofsky *Krinsky*!" The egg-shaped woman corrected her.

The women squealed and embraced. The egg-shaped man shrugged his shoulders helplessly at Charlie. "I went to Mumford."

Charlie shrugged back and moved toward the no-host bar, hoping for a friendly familiar face or at least a healthy shot of Tequila. He felt like a loser.

Metal Mouth Felch had warned him. "The only ones that will show up are the people we hated in high school, and they'll do nothing but stick it to you, Fish. Screw 'em."

Metal Mouth had decided not to come to the reunion for good reason. He'd turned into a cocktail lounge drunk by night and a door-to-door aluminum siding scam artist working for a small-time East-side Mafioso by day. He had lost contact with all his high school buddies except Charlie. He had borrowed from all of them, except Charlie, who had no money to lend.

Although he hadn't degenerated to the depths of Metal Mouth Felch, Charlie's life wasn't much to brag about.

"Hey, Gefilte Fish! What the hell kept ya? I got a brewski here with your name on it!" Joe Murphy's booming voice could be heard across the crowd. He was belly-up to the no-host bar, and appeared to be as buzzed as Charlie. Although he was dressed in a conservative charcoal gray suit, it did little to offset the shock value of his two-toned platinum-blonde-and-black wrestler hair. Charlie threaded his way to the bar.

"I thought you weren't gonna show, Joe."

"Nah. I figured that it'd be a real goof to laugh at all these pencil-necks and pear-bodies. Look at 'em. Not an original thought in this room. They bought the goddamn program. So be glad you're a freak, Fish. I know I am."

"We're not freaks. We're masochists. I'm getting the hell outta here."

"Hello, Charlie," said a gentle female voice.

He turned to see Judy Weinstein. She smiled warmly at

him. If possible, she was even more beautiful. Her skin was smoother. Her blue eyes were more luminous. Her black hair was longer, thicker, and more lustrous. She touched his forearm and lightly kissed his cheek. He felt as if his heart might stop.

He still loved her, his junior high homecoming date. "Judy." Her name gasped out of his mouth.

They hugged. He closed his eyes. It felt like spontaneous combustion.

"Hey, Fish! That's my wife you're groping!" chuckled a male voice that he knew all too well. Charlie opened his eyes.

David Rothman stood there, a smug grin on his face and a proprietary hand on Judy Weinstein's shoulder. He appeared wealthy and dignified in a well-tailored black pin-striped three-piece Brooks Brothers suit. Charlie felt sick to his guts. He moved away from Judy. Rothman stuck out his hand for a shake. Against his better judgement, Charlie shook David Rothman's hand. The shake was cold and brief. A "fuck you" handshake. A "the better man won" handshake. "So what are you up to these days, Fish?"

"I'm an architect," he lied.

Rothman's eyebrows lifted. "Oh really? I'm impressed."

Charlie decided not to ask any personal questions of David Rothman. Of course, he didn't have to.

Rothman's chin raised in a Mussolini-like defiance, his body straightened to emphasize the two or three inch height difference between him and Charlie, and his mouth twisted into a strange, almost beatific smile. "I am a rabbi." These few words were said in a resonant mellifluous David Rothman voice that Charlie had never heard before; a cultivated voice that might be heard on the *bimah* of a suburban reformed temple.

Charlie felt cold inside. He wanted to smash a cream pie in Rothman's self-satisfied pompous face Soupy Sales-style like in the old "Three Bs" days, but he was an adult and he had to maintain a veneer of civility.

Rothman draped his arm around Judy's shoulders and pulled her close to him. She blushed and looked away from Charlie. She knew that he was hurting.

"So where are you living these days, Fish?" asked Rothman.

"Right here."

"I didn't know that you lived in the St. Regis." Rothman chuckled at his own bad joke.

"Yeah. I live in the penthouse." He clenched his fists.

Rothman guffawed meanly, betraying his refined surface. "That's funny, Fish. You always were funny. Jude and I live in Manhattan. My temple is on Fifth Avenue, not far from the art museums. Stephen Wise was once the rabbi there. We love New York City. Detroit is just too small and provincial for us, isn't it, dear?"

She smiled apologetically at Charlie. "I need to pay a visit to the little girls' room, so if you boys will excuse me." She pulled away from her husband and shot him a subtle dirty look as she walked away.

"Women. Can't live with 'em. Can't . . . well, you know the rest," chuckled Rothman.

"You don't know what you have," said Charlie, but Rothman didn't hear him. He had moved on to a conversation with *Dr.* Seymour Marcus, once known as "The Mooch."

Charlie squeezed next to Joe Murphy at the no-host bar. "Religion is the opiate of the assholes," he muttered.

"Hey, Gefilte Fish. I'm getting' a head start on you!"

"Not for long." He'd need tequila to kill the pain in his guts and in his heart.

Charlie found a chair behind a potted plastic palm tree, an ideal location where he could stay hidden and sneak a peek at the reunion crowd. He was feeling the tequila buzz.

Joe Murphy was up in Psycho Bobby Shapiro's hotel room hoovering lines of coke. Charlie wasn't into coke, or any other drug that made him feel stupid. Psycho Bobby was selling the white powder for a living.

"Charlie Fish! Is that you? Holy shit! You're not fat anymore . . . and neither am I!" shouted a drunken female voice behind him. A small hand smacked him hard between his shoulder blades. Nancee Gordon stood next to his chair, smiling brightly. She was the funniest girl in school and one of the fattest. Charlie looked up at her and couldn't believe what he was seeing. She was at least seventy pounds slimmer than he had remembered her. She was gorgeous—round and soft in all the right places, as only an ex-fatgirl could be. Charlie and Nancee had been Platonic friends in their senior year at OPHS. They had collaborated on the Oak Park High School Class of 1964 senior skit that would end all Oak Park High senior class skits for eternity. The "official" script that they had submitted to Vice Principal Artunian was an innocuous sendup of "The Wizard of Oz." Unknown to the school administration, there was a second "unofficial" script that was a vicious, subversive, and demented spoof of "The Wizard of Oz." Charlie and Nancee spent hours in his basement laughing their asses off as they cooked up both scripts.

The "unofficial" script was performed during graduation week and seen by students, parents, and faculty on the Oak Park High auditorium stage. Charlie kneeled on his shoes as he portrayed a lecherous munchkin that bore more than a passing resemblance to Mr. Rademacher, the autocratic five-foot-tall shop teacher. Nancee Gordon played the Wicked

Witch of the West like Mrs. O'Shaughnessy the shrill ditsy guidance counselor. Other students played thinly disguised teachers and faculty. Howieschultz played the Wizard as Principal Blechman, complete with a flesh-toned rubber swim cap baldpate. Blow jobs, excessive drinking, cigarette smoking, drag racing, and other forbidden pleasures were woven into the plotline. Most parents and faculty members left the auditorium en masse. Students roared with laughter and gave the cast a ten-minute standing ovation and two encores.

Ten years later, Charlie couldn't take his eyes off his former collaborator Nancee Gordon.

"I don't know about you, Charlie, but this reunion is a drag. Do you wanna get the fuck outta here?"

"Hell, yes!"

Charlie and Nancee spent the rest of the night in Windsor, Ontario, at the Elmwood Casino Nightclub, where they saw comedian Jackie Mason. A dreary evening had turned into a perfect one. Charlie and Nancee screamed with laughter at Jackie Mason's schmaltz herring life observations.

After the show, they went back to Charlie's apartment and humped like wild animals.

Three months later, they were married.

• 1976 •

CELIA Fish's head rested on Nancee's shoulder. She had fallen asleep. She looked almost peaceful. Celia loved Nancee.

sitting shiva

Charlie and Nancee had run out of conversation. They knew each other too well, for better or worse.

There was no chance of reconciliation for them even if they had wanted it. She had moved to Somerset, a new swinging-singles apartment complex development in suburban Rochester. She was teaching full-time at an affluent all-white private elementary school in Birmingham, a contrast to her old teaching job at inner city Detroit's Central High School. Charlie felt personally responsible for killing off her idealism.

He stared at her as she made quiet small talk with his Aunt Beatrice. The worry lines that had begun to crease her forehead when they lived together had disappeared. Living poor with Charlie had taken a toll. She now looked content.

The doorbell rang. Charlie went to the door. His old grade school nemesis, Borlack the cop, stood there. He had packed on thirty pounds—all in his gut—and his trademark handlebar mustache had turned white. "Is this the Fish residence?" he asked. He appeared not to recognize Charlie. Almost twenty years had passed since the schoolhouse-defacing incident, Charlie's last encounter with him.

"Can I help you?" Charlie tried not to reveal any trace of intimidation in his voice.

"I'm looking for a Mrs. Celia Fish." He stepped inside.

"I'm her son. Is there a problem?"

Seeing that the apartment was filled with people, Borlack hesitated, then spoke in low tones. "She reported some phone death threats."

Charlie felt dizzy. He leaned a shoulder against the door-jamb. Maybe his mother wasn't lying about the phone calls. Was Antoinette Abboud still alive, he wondered?

Nancee walked to the door. "Charlie, is anything wrong?"

"Family business. I'll take care of it," he said curtly to her. She flinched, realizing with a twinge of pain that she was no longer a part of the family.

"This is something that the police should deal with, Mr. Fish," said Borlack.

"I've been talking to you cops for years about this, and for years you haven't done shit. I said, I'll take care of it." He brushed past the burly cop and exited the apartment, slamming the door behind him. The abrupt sound jolted his mother awake.

"What's going on?" she whimpered.

"That's what I'd like to know," grumbled Borlack the cop.

∵

MURDEROUS anger and fear surged through Charlie's body as he ran down Parklawn Street. Nancee ran after him. "Charlie, what's wrong?" she shouted.

"It's my problem, Nancee!" he shouted over his shoulder, then ran faster. He knew that her chain smoking would wind her.

"Goddamn it! You're in no shape to drive! I'll drive you!" she shouted after him. When they were married, his driving scared her. She hated his erratic make-your-own-rules driving style. She'd always drive.

He turned to her. "I'm not your headache anymore, Nancee," he shouted, enunciating each word.

His words hit her like a fist. Her eyes filled with tears. She slowed down to a stop.

∵

CHARLIE floored the Bumblebee. It sped down Third at seventy, thirty-five miles over the speed limit. Highland Park cops were notorious for pulling over and browbeating blacks and longhaired whites like Charlie. Once he had spent a night in a Highland Park police station jail cell for driving without a license. The next morning they let him make his one phone call, and Nancee brought his license and bail money. Charlie was now too angry to be afraid of the Highland Park police and the threat of a night or two in the pokey.

As he neared Piggins Street, he took his foot off the accelerator, slowing the car down to twenty-five miles below the speed limit. He still remembered where Antoinette Abboud lived. Although he had lived only a mile away from her for the past five years, he'd always avoided driving down Third.

A truck blasted its horn as it swerved around him. "Speed up, asshole!" screamed the truckdriver. Charlie ignored him. Although there was a No Stopping sign, he pulled the car over to the right curb, causing even more horns to blast at him. He stared across the street at what was left of

Antoinette Abboud's house: a foundation and mounds of rubble surrounded by a chickenwire construction fence. A "Giacometti Salvage Company" sign was on the fence.

Was she dead? Charlie wondered.

His feelings ricocheted from sad to angry to helpless. A Detroit city bus blasted its horn at him. "Fuck you!" he screamed and jammed the stick-shift into first gear, causing the little Datsun to lurch forward amd screech into Third Street traffic. "Fuck all of you! Fuck the world!"

· 1963 ·

CHARLIE couldn't sleep. He couldn't live with what he had seen in Highland Park eight hours earlier. Antoinette Abboud's frenetic hate-filled phone voice had haunted his dreams for years. Now there was a face to go with it. In his dreams, her thick make-up contorted her face into a crazed clown's grimace. He wanted her out of his dreams forever.

Charlie sat up in bed. He crept out of his bedroom. The floor creaked as he tiptoed past his parents' bedroom. He didn't want to wake them. He especially didn't want to deal with his father. He wondered how his father could love a sick disgusting beast like Antoinette Abboud.

He went into the living room thinking that watching "Mr. X" on Shock Theater, WXYZ's late-night weekend horror movie show, might put him to sleep. "Captive Wild Woman," a laughable Forties B-horror flick starring John Carradine, Milburn Stone, and Evelyn "the Queen of Scream" Ankers was on. Ankers was almost as sexy as Gayle Sondergaard the Spiderwoman. Charlie probably milked a gallon of jism out of his dick watching Gayle Sondergaard creating evil on Shock Theater. He turned on the TV. On screen, the American flag flapped in the breeze as Frank Sinatra sang "I Can't Get Started with You," WXYZ's nightly station sign-off. He tried the three other television stations. They had already signed off. "Shit," he said to himself a little too loud. He turned off the television. He saw his father's money clip and keys in an ashtray on the lamp table next to the TV. A gambler's wad of greenbacks was in the clip. He picked up the wad, and pulled it out of the clip. He spread the bills across the couch. He counted out ten one hundred dollar bills, six fifties, six tens, and one two dollar bill. His father had always said that the two dollar bill was for "good luck." Charlie pocketed the two dollar bill. He grabbed the ring of keys, and pocketed them as well. He headed for the front door, opened it, and stepped onto the front porch. The moon couldn't be seen. The sky was illuminated only by stars. The cement felt cold on his bare feet. The cool summer night breeze felt good on his skin through the thin layer of pajamas.

He stepped off the porch and walked to his father's recently Simonized Olds 98 that was parked in the driveway. He pulled out the ring of keys and found the silver GM key. He unlocked the driver door and slid inside. Even though his father had bought the car several months ago, the smell of glove leather was still strong. An opened Kool cigarette pack was on the passenger seat. Charlie picked up the pack, pulled out a cigarette, and put it in his mouth. He

pushed in the cigarette lighter. He had never smoked a cigarette. The lighter popped out of its socket. Charlie lit the
cigarette, sucking down the smoke, as he had seen his father
and the Eagle Dairy hoods do. The stream of smoke seared
his throat and fogged his lungs. He choked on and hacked
out the excess smoke for a full thirty seconds.
"Sonofabitch!" he coughed out these words, jammed the
key into the ignition, and turned it. The engine roared, a
sound louder than he had intended. His heart beat quickly.
None of the lights in his parents' house or in the neighbors'
houses turned on. He had never started a car. He had never
driven a car. He grabbed the automatic transmission
gearshift lever and pulled it to "R," as he had seen his father
do. He stepped on the accelerator pedal too hard, sending
the Olds down the driveway and into the street. The Olds'
back bumper slammed into the high curb across the street,
in front of the Rabinowitz's house. A light flicked on in the
Rabinowitz's bedroom. Cold fearful sweat beaded on his
forehead. He shifted into "Drive" and pressed the accelerator petal, this time with less force. The silver Olds proceed-
ed cautiously down Westridge Street.

Although he stopped too long at stop signs and red lights,
stomped on the brakes a bit too hard, and didn't stay strictly
within the lane lines, he was driving well. Six months earlier,
he had flunked driver's ed. Coolidge turned into Schaeffer
Road as he entered the Detroit city limits. He turned on the
radio and found WCHB. Garnet Mims was singing "Cry!
Cry! Baby!"

He tried to remember how to get to the John Lodge

Expressway. After driving down Schaeffer for about a half hour, he realized that the neighborhood was unfamiliar. Everyone on the street and in passing cars was black. He turned the radio volume up. The Duo-tones' "Shake Your Tailfeather" blasted. He turned down Davison. He had heard of that street. Dexter and Davison used to be the heart of the old Jewish neighborhood. He had lived in this neighborhood until he was five. He passed the Avalon Theater. It was boarded up. Although he remembered very little from those years, he remembered the four-hour Saturday matinee "cartoon carnivals" at the Avalon. His parents would always talk about Fredson's and Boesky's delis, the Jewish neighborhood hangouts. They had long been replaced by rib-and-shrimp joints.

He saw Clements Avenue, the street where he and his father had lived with his grandfather Nosanchuk for the first five years of his life while his mother was in the tuberculosis sanitorium. He turned left. The street was narrow and dark. Most of the streetlights were either broken or shot out. Many of the apartment buildings and brownstones were no more than burned-out unrepaired shells. He didn't know if he could find his grandfather's duplex or what remained of it. He could only remember that it was in the middle of the block and had had a dark blue awning and a yellow brick facade. He remembered being on the losing end of a fist-fight with another five-year-old. He remembered his father screaming from the porch, "Hit him! Hit him back, or I'll hit you!" He remembered crying and running away from the fight.

He stopped in front of a duplex with a yellow brick facade but no awning. Car headlight high-beams flashed on behind him, the reflection in the rear view mirror almost blinding him. He yelped in fear.

"Move your goddamn ass, white boy!" shouted a drunk voice.

Charlie turned to see a primer-black 1957 Chevy behind him. The driver stuck his head out the window. He wore a nylon do-rag over his conk. Charlie could see the outlines of two other men in the Chevy. He jammed on the accelerator and laid rubber down Clements. After several hairpin turns, he saw a green Davison Expressway sign. He made a sharp left onto the expressway entrance. The Davison Expressway was only a quarter-mile long, one of the first expressways in the country. It led right to the John Lodge. There were very few cars on the Lodge. A large green expressway sign said, "Third Street, Highland Park, One Mile." Only then did he remember where he really wanted to go. He could see Antoinette Abboud's fat ugly face in his mind. He took the Third Street exit.

The Contours sang "First I Look at the Purse," a kick-ass party song. At 2:00 in the morning there was no traffic on Third Street. He pressed the accelerator pedal flat. The Olds engine roared to its top end. Charlie imagined smashing the car into her fat body, hearing her shriek like a slaughtered hog, and making her as terrified as she had made him and his mother for all these years.

He turned off the car radio as he approached her house. The lamp was turned on in her living room picture window as it had been on the day when he and Joe Murphy had waited in hiding for a first glimpse of Antoinette Abboud. He parked in front of the house. He didn't care if she saw him. He got out of the car and walked to the house. He pushed through a tall shrub to get a closer view of the living room, nearly tripping over a large chunk of concrete that had chipped off the front porch.

He stood on his tiptoes and peered inside. The television was tuned in to a station test pattern. Charlie could see a flabby arm dangling over the side of the couch. His guts turned with fear and anger. He stared at the arm. He wanted to pull it out of its socket. She had probably either fallen asleep or passed out while watching television. A large metal ashtray filled with cigarette butts was on the lamp table next to her arm. He hoped that she would get lung cancer. He surveyed every inch of the room. It was a filthy disgusting mess. It looked like his neighbor Old Brady the Wino's living room. Several half-empty beer bottles and a plate of half-eaten egg foo young were on a coffee table. Kid's toys were strewn all over the floor. Articles of dirty clothing were draped over every chair. If possible, Charlie began to feel sorry for her. He hated himself for feeling this way. Tears ran down his face.

"Goddamn bitch!" he shouted and turned to walk away. He fell over the chunk of concrete, ripping open his pants at the right knee and flattening the shrub. Blood flowed from a cut on his shin. He scrambled to his feet and kicked the chunk as hard as he could. Pain shot through his big toe.

"Fuck you, Antoinette!" he screamed. He picked up the concrete chunk and heaved it over his head and into the picture window. It exploded loudly into shards of glass. Charlie yelped in fear and stumbled backwards out of the shrubs.

He could hear Antoinette Abboud's terrified shrieks coming from inside her living room; they were piercing, inhuman sounds like a wounded animal. "Leave my mother alone, Antoinette, or I'll kill you and your children!" he screamed at the smashed window.

Lights flicked on in nearby apartments. Charlie ran to his car, flung open the door, and scrambled into the driver's seat. He turned the key in the ignition. The engine stalled twice, then started with an angry roar. The Olds fishtailed down Third, its headlights off. He jammed his elbow onto his car horn, creating one loud long farewell blast.

He knew that she would never terrorize his mother again.

• 1976 •

AT EIGHT P.M., Charlie entered his mother's apartment. He was carrying two large supermarket-sized brown bags filled with white cartons of Chinese food from the Rikshaw Inn. The living room was dark except for the picture-frame light that illuminated the large oil painting of Charlie Fish as "the bar mitzvah boy" posing somberly in a white shirt, tie, navy-blue suit jacket, and prayer shawl. There were no people in the living room other than his mother. She sat in her wheelchair in the center of the room. She stared into space.

To Charlie, she looked emotionally drained. She glanced at him without expression. "Hello, mother," he said as he set the bags down on a low coffee table. "Where is everyone?"

"I sent them all home. I have a headache," she answered in a voice that was only barely above a whisper.

"I brought food."

"I'm not hungry."

"It's from the Rikshaw Inn. Your favorite. Enough food for ten people. What am I gonna do with all this food?"

"I don't care," she said this without looking at him.

"Have there been any more of those crazy phone calls?'

"No."

"She's dead, mother. I went by her house today. They tore it down."

"I know she's not dead." She folded her arms stubbornly across her chest. "I don't want to talk about it anymore."

"Okay, mother. I don't want to upset you," he sighed. He was sure that she was lying about the phone calls from Antoinette Abboud to get attention. He was sure that the maniac was dead.

He pulled white cartons from the bags, announcing each one as he set them on the table and opened the tops. "I got shrimp with lobster sauce, Steak Kow, almond boneless chicken, fried rice. Everything that you love. Mmmmm," he said teasingly. He could tell that the smell of the food was getting to her.

"Shrimp isn't kosher," she snarled.

"Since when does a shrimp have cloven hooves?"

"Shrimp is shellfish. What's the matter with you?"

"I won't tell if you don't tell," Charlie said with a wink.

"Get it out of here. Where's your respect?" she growled at him.

He was glad to finally get a rise out of her. He pulled paper plates and plastic forks out of a bag.

"Oh, Mother, by the way, I forgot to tell you. I have almond pressed duck, your very favorite," he said this with a teasing lilt in his voice as he opened the last carton on the table. He could tell that she was hungrier than she was letting on.

"I told you that I don't want you or this food here!" she said this loudly and distinctly.

"Okay. You win. I'll get rid of the shrimp in lobster sauce." He picked up the carton of shrimp and walked to the kitchen. He dumped the food into the sink, and turned on the water and the garbage disposal. The shrimp in lobster sauce formed a yellow whirlpool as it sucked down into the drain. The grinding of the disposal blades was a loud angry sound that matched his mood. He saw the faces of his father, Antoinette Abboud, Peter Abboud, and his mother swirling into the drain along with the shrimp in lobster sauce.

When he returned to the living room, Charlie saw that his mother had set up a plate of Chinese food on the coffee table. She had a second plate of Chinese food on her lap. She was noisily wolfing down the food without a thought of table etiquette. He was shocked. Social graces had always been the center of his mother's life.

sitting shiva

Charlie sat down at the coffee table, picked up a plastic fork, and speared a hunk of almond boneless chicken.

∴

AFTER dinner, Charlie drove to his apartment on Gladstone. He hadn't been back since the funeral. He parked behind a wheel-less 1948 Dodge on cement blocks, one of many car bodies deposited within a three-block area by his neighbor Elmore the junkman. Charlie unlocked the building's front door. The super had finally fixed the lock. He stepped over a puddle of piss in the vestibule and went to the rows of mailboxes. He opened the cubicle window labeled "Fish" and pulled out a week's accumulation of mail. As he dragged through the decaying lobby and walked toward his apartment he thumbed through the envelopes, mostly separating the junk mail from bills. He stopped at one envelope.

"To Charlie" was hand-printed in shaky childlike block letters on the envelope's face. He recognized his father's writing. A sixth-grade dropout, Morris Fish was barely literate. "June 10, 1976" was the postmark on the envelope—the day before the police found Morris Fish.

Charlie felt headache pains. He unlocked his apartment and flicked on a light. He could hear mice scrambling for cover. He sat on his threadbare couch, exhaled, gritted his teeth, and opened the envelope. As he pulled out the one folded sheet of paper, a small key fell out. He picked it up and examined it. The number "134" was etched into it. As he

unfolded the letter, his heart hammered in his chest like a
Ginger Baker drum solo.

To Charlie

National Bank of Detroit next to Produce Club.
Box 134 C. Your name on the account. Do not
tell your mother.

Love always

Dad

Charlie crumpled the letter into a ball, and flushed it
down the toilet. He grabbed his pants, removed his wallet,
and shoved the key into one of the small leather sleeves. He
wondered if his father had more nightmares and secrets for
him, delivered from beyond the grave.

∵

sixth day
of shiva

· 1976 ·

CHARLIE arrived at the National Bank of Detroit at 10:00 A.M., opening time. Although the morning was unusually cool for late summer, sweat beaded on his forehead as he sat at the bank officer's desk waiting for him to retrieve his wake-up mug of coffee. The sign on the desk said "Don Wattles, Assistant Branch Manager."

Wattles smiled apologetically as he returned to his desk. A Jed Clampett lookalike decked out in a Robert Hall suit and clip-on Rooster tie, he was out of place in this bank branch with its mostly black clientele and staff. He handed Charlie a form on a clipboard. "Sign here please, Mr. Fish. I'll also need to see a driver's license."

After Charlie obediently followed the instructions, Wattles took his safety deposit box key, led him to a room with a gate, and buzzed him inside.

Charlie's heart beat rapidly as the bank officer searched up and down the rows of safety deposit boxes for "134C." He unlocked the small door with his own key and Charlie's, and pulled out the long metal box. He handed it to Charlie. The box felt cold in his hands.

"If you'd like, Mr. Fish, you can use one of the private booths." The bank officer pointed at a short corridor adjacent to the room.

Charlie nodded politely at "Mr. Don Wattles, Assistant Bank Manager," and selected an unoccupied booth, shutting the door tightly behind him. The tiny room consisted of a swivel chair, a wall shelf table, and a crookneck lamp. He set the box on the table, exhaled sharply, and sat down.

He opened the box's metal lid. A large manila envelope and a white letter-sized envelope were inside. Charlie opened the smaller envelope and pulled out two folded pages. He felt a dull throbbing pain in his temple.

His father's handwriting was a childlike scrawl.

Dear Charlie

You know I love you and your mother more than my own life. And I hate what my life is. Its my own dam fault. I owe money to peopel. They says there going to kill me if I don't pay. You and your mother should not pay. Open the big envelop. Its for your mother. Its card game money I been putting aside.

Charlie picked up the large manila envelope. It felt heavy in his hands. He ripped it open. Short stacks of hundred-dollar bills held together by rubber bands fell out onto the shelf-table with several dull thumps. His heart pounded as he picked up one of the bundles. He counted twenty hundred-dollar bills. He laid the money bundles on the tables. There were thirty bundles in front of him, each appearing to contain the same amount of currency. "Sixty thousand dollars," he mumbled to himself. Sweat rolled down his face.

He picked up the letter again. His hand trembled. He continued reading it.

> Tell your mother not tell nobody not even famly. She should maybe move away. Take a thousand for you Charlie and use it wise. Don't be like me. I must tell you the truth. You have a brother Peter. He is a good boy not like his mother a bad woman. He wants to meet you. Maybe I'm a cowerd running away from troubel. I know I called you that but your braver than I ever was. Don't be like me.
>
> Love always. Dad

He slid his hand deep into the manila envelope to check for any additional message from his father. He pulled out a grainy yellowing black-and-white photo from the Fifties. It was taken at Knotts Berry Farm in California. Six-year-old Charlie posed with his parents next to a seven-foot-tall wooden Indian chief. They were all smiling natural, unposed smiles. The trip to California was the only time he could remember being totally happy in his parents' company—the only time that he could remember his parents spending an entire week together without one fight.

· 1953 ·

CHARLIE couldn't believe that his father had actually made good on his promise to take him and his mother on a trip to Los Angeles.

Palm trees were everywhere, there were six channels on the TV, and the weather was warm in January. To Charlie, it was paradise, a dream come true.

His father's third cousin, Shep the movie producer, was throwing his son Lawrence a fancy bar mitzvah at the Beverly Wilshire Hotel. This was the reason for the Fishes' visit.

Cousin Shep lived in a big house in Coldwater Canyon. He told bad jokes, swore a lot, and bragged about playing golf with his neighbor Danny Thomas, a fellow Detroiter who also made good in Hollywood. He bought Charlie ten twenty-five-cent comic books, which rankled his mother no end. She would only let him buy one ten-cent comic book a month at Hammerstein's drugstore, if he was lucky. Comics were the ultimate source of serious mind-rot, in the opinion of Celia Fish; but she didn't complain. Cousin Shep the movie producer, his "fancy blonde Social Register *shiksa* wife," and their sprawling home impressed her.

Charlie liked him.

His father liked him too. They were almost equally matched at pinochle. Cousin Shep had arranged games for both of them with "rich Hollywood suckers" at the Hillcrest Country Club.

Charlie and his parents stayed at a cheap motel, the Rancho Vista, on Wilshire Boulevard in the Fairfax District near the stuffed dinosaurs at the LaBrea Tar Pits and the restaurant shaped like a Laurel and Hardy hat.

On his second day in California, Charlie became violently ill. His jaw swelled up, causing his face to look like a chipmunk's. Cold chills surged through his body, even though it was seventy degrees outside the motel room. His mother piled blankets on top of him. Cousin Shep's wife Betty sent over the family doctor for a housecall. The doctor's diagnosis: Charlie had the mumps.

Since his mother had never had the mumps, she had to keep her distance from him. His father chose to become his nurse, not unusual because he was "mother and father" to Charlie while Celia was in the TB hospital only a few years earlier. Morris had to cancel his much-anticipated card game at the Hillcrest, and he'd never canceled a pinochle game with rich suckers.

For two days, every inch of Charlie's body ached. While his mother went out sightseeing with friends and family, Charlie and his father were cooped up in the Rancho Vista Motel room. His father kept giving him glasses of orange juice. He couldn't eat solid foods without puking. His father kept feeding dimes into the pay-TV set. They snuggled together in the bed, and laughed at Tom Terrific, Pixie and Dixie, and Crusader Rabbit cartoons.

After Charlie's fever broke, his father and Cousin Shep took him to Hollywood and treated him to a C.C. Brown's bittersweet hot fudge sundae, and then to a movie at the famous Grauman's Chinese Theater. Ava Gardner and Clark Gable starred in "Mogambo," an African jungle picture. Charlie liked jungle movies. He liked Ava Gardner's beautiful heart-shaped face. Later, Cousin Shep told him that he knew Ava Gardner.

• 1976 •

CHARLIE drove down Michigan Avenue, Dearborn's main drag. He'd only go near Dearborn to visit Greenfield Village and the Henry Ford Museum, the auto magnate's love song to the Industrial Revolution. Although he enjoyed seeing the old cars, President Lincoln's Ford Theater seat, complete with blood stains, and Thomas Edison's lab, imported brick-by-brick, test-tube-by-test-tube from New Jersey, Dearborn held nothing but bad vibes for him. He had long heard of signs on Dearborn suburban lawns proclaiming "no Jews, dogs, or niggers."

Longtime Dearborn mayor Orville Hubbard, hand-picked by old man Ford himself, made sure that blacks never crossed the city line from neighboring Inkster into Dearborn. Jews owned a few Michigan Avenue clothes and furniture stores, but none were allowed to reside in the pristine Dearborn neighborhoods.

Charlie's father used to tell him how, back in the Thirties, he'd go to Dearborn with some *shtarker* buddies to break up German-American Bund meetings with fists and lead pipes. He told Charlie about how the Dearborn *Independent* would run installments of old Henry Ford's virulently anti-Semitic book "The International Jew."

Charlie remembered going to Metropolitan Beach with friends, and sneaking into the cordoned-off-for-residents-only Dearborn City Beach area, where the sand seemed much whiter and the girls seemed much prettier than the ones who sunbathed in the less exclusive parts of Metro. He remembered being hustled off the City Beach by security guards who were actually off-duty Dearborn cops.

Now Charlie hoped that the Dearborn cops wouldn't pull him over. It would be hard to explain the sixty thousand dollars stuffed into his pants and jockey shorts for safekeeping.

Dearborn was a Ford Motor Company town created for executives and skilled workers. In recent years, large numbers of Syrians and Lebanese had moved into the older areas of the city, a demographic fact that caused much controversy among the City Fathers. Peter Abboud was one of the newcomers.

Charlie consulted his crude hand-drawn map and turned right on Lexington, Peter's street. Most of the homes were two-story colonials with manicured lawns large enough to be tended by riding mowers. Unlike most of the other houses on the street, there was no black jockey statue in front of Peter Abboud's house. Charlie pulled The Bumblebee into the circular driveway behind two new Ford station wagons. He felt intimidated. He'd been floundering for years while his younger long-lost half-brother had it all: the family and the house in the suburbs.

For a moment, he felt like driving away; but then the front door opened. Peter stepped onto the porch, a big welcoming grin on his face. "Hey, Charlie!" he called out.

Charlie waved back weakly. He grabbed his house gift, a family-sized jug of Cribari—a cheap yet respectable Italian red wine—and climbed out of the car.

Peter hopped off the porch and squeezed him in a bearhug. "Glad you could make it, Charlie."

Peter steered him inside the house. Although the exterior was a traditional colonial similar to other houses on Lexington, the interior was open and dramatic. The winding handcrafted wooden staircase with exquisitely carved handrails was the centerpiece of the house. Charlie couldn't take his eyes off it. "It's beautiful," he said.

"Thanks. Built it myself." Peter smiled with pride.

"The handrails too?"

"Carved 'em myself. It took forever."

"So, you're an artist too."

"I tell the squares that I'm in construction, but I'm a master carpenter. The wife here runs the business. I'd be broke if it wasn't for her."

Georgia Abboud was in the living room picking up children's toys from the floor. She looked up and greeted him with a tight smile and wary eyes. "Please excuse the mess."

Georgia was attractive in a homey housewife way with a short blonde pageboy and denim gardening clothes. Despite the casual appearance, there was a well-bred formality about her. She walked over to Charlie and extended her hand for a shake. "Pleased to meet you."

The shake was brief. Her hand was cold. She scanned his attire, the bright chaotic Hawaiian shirt, bleach-spotted jeans, and threadbare sneakers. Her expression only barely hid her slight feelings of revulsion. "Would you like something to drink?" she said with a thin smile.

Charlie smiled back at her and displayed the jug of Cribari wine. "Oh, I almost forgot that I brought this."

She stared at the bottle, horrified as if it were hillbilly moonshine. She took the jug from Charlie, grunted and almost doubled over from the weight of the heavy glass jug. "Thank you, Charlie," she said stiffly, "Dinner will be ready in about an hour."

Peter aimed a sharp stare at her. "We'll have Charlie's wine with dinner."

She blinked hard at Peter's remark. She turned and walked toward the kitchen, holding the heavy jug in both hands. "Nice meeting you, Charlie," Georgia Abboud said over her shoulder.

"Don't mind her. She'll warm up once she gets to know you. She's very protective of me. C'mon, have a brewski with me," said Peter, beckoning Charlie to follow him.

They went downstairs to a room that was obviously Peter Abboud's sanctuary. There was a poker table, several Laz-E-Boy chairs, and a big-screen TV for the benefit of his poker buddies. The walls were paneled with birdseye maple, and the floors were covered with handmade American Indian rugs. Charlie knew that he could live in this room for the rest of his life. He sat in a Laz-E-Boy and reclined back. Peter opened a cabinet door under the big-screen TV, revealing a small refrigerator. He pulled out two bottles of Upper Canada beer and two frosty mugs from the freezer compartment. "This was the old man's favorite room, Charlie. He'd come over and you couldn't get him to budge out of this room."

"Did he come over here a lot?"

"I didn't see Dad that much as a kid, but after the grandchildren happened, he was here all the time." Peter handed him a mug of beer. "Now you're here. Life is funny. It took the old man dying to bring us together."

"When you were a kid, were you jealous of me?" he blurted out these words and immediately regretted them.

Peter sat in the La-Z-Boy next to Charlie. "I'd be lying if I didn't say yes. My old lady filled my head with poison. She always talked about how you lived in a nice house in the suburbs, while we lived in a Highland Park shit-hole. She talked about how you always had new toys, and me and my brothers and sisters got crummy hand-me-downs. Sometimes she'd drive us by your house. I was jealous, but the jealousy made me want to succeed."

"Are you still jealous of me?"

"A little. The old man used to talk about you a lot. You had the fancy bar mitzvah. You were the big genius. Yeah, he used to call you 'the genius.' I always felt like I'd never be able to live up to that."

A loud laugh burst out of Charlie's mouth, a bitter guffaw that surprised him and Peter Abboud. "The old man bragged about *me?*"

"All the time."

"But I was the klutz that dropped the baseball. I was the idiot that got straight Ds on his report card. I was the drug addict slob that didn't give him grandchildren. I'm the one that should be jealous of you. You gave him everything that he wanted. I gave him nothing."

"You have his name, Charlie. I'm the bastard. I'll always be the bastard."

"Jesus, lighten up. The old man did a number on both of us."

"Yeah. As soon as I started making decent money, I found a good shrink. I always knew that I needed one. I mostly worked through a lot of shit about the old man and my mother."

"Your mother," Charlie said quietly and inhaled sharply.

"She was a real piece of work back then, Charlie."

"She went way beyond being a piece of work. Do you know what she did to me and my mother?"

"I know some of it."

"Do you know how she scared my mother shitless? How she scared me when I was just a little kid?" he took a big swig of beer.

"Yes. My mother's crazy, Charlie. She's always been crazy. She fucked up me and the other kids royally. My brothers and sisters all became alcoholics or druggies. I'm the middle one and the strongest. I always knew that I was fucked up. I think realizing that is step one to unfucking yourself. So I dumped out my hate, got religion—I'm a Catholic—I learned to forgive Mom and Dad. I learned to forgive you."

"You forgave me? You didn't know me."

Peter stood up. "I want to show you something."

He went to the built-in bookshelves filled with paper-backs and coffee-table art books. He pulled out a leather-bound photo album and handed it to Charlie. "I put this together just for you. We have years to catch up on."

Charlie pushed the La-Z-Boy into an upright position. His pulse fluttered nervously as he opened the album. On page one was a formally posed recent photo of Peter's family. Charlie guessed that they were dressed in their Easter church clothes. Peter was wearing the same dark suit that Charlie saw him wearing at his father's funeral. Georgia was beautiful, without a hint of domestic fatigue, in her pastel pink Saks Fifth Avenue dress. Peter and Georgia posed arm in arm, a genuine loving couple. Charlie felt a twinge of jealousy and hated himself for it. A sweetly smiling, pretty blonde eight-year old girl, and an unsmiling, curly-haired brunette five-year old boy posed in front of their parents. Charlie was drawn to the boy's face, particularly the intensity of his brown eyes. "That's Pete Junior. He looks like our old man, doesn't he? Acts like him, too. A stubborn charming pain in the ass," laughed Peter. "Camille is a dead ringer for her mother. Like her mother, she refers to me and Junior as 'the children.'"

Charlie couldn't stop staring at Pete Junior's face. He turned the page to another family portrait: Antoinette Abboud's family, circa 1959, he guessed. It was a black-and-white photo with a crease down the center. Peter was close to Pete Junior's age. Charlie recognized the living room of the Highland Park house. Six people, Antoinette and her five children, were gathered in front of an aluminum Christmas tree loaded with too many plastic ornaments. He guessed that she was in her late twenties when the picture was taken. She was slim and almost attractive in a cheap available way. He understood his father's physical attraction to her. Charlie had been attracted to women like her.

"Are those your brothers and sisters?" he asked.

"Yep. The whole Abboud brood."

Charlie stared at the innocent young faces in the photo. "Are any of them related to me?"

"No. My brothers and sisters each had a different father. None were as generous as our dad was." Peter's voice quivered with emotion. "He wasn't all bad, Charlie."

"I know that."

"Underneath all the bullshit he was a good guy."

"He tried to be," he said bitterly and turned the page to a photo of Peter as an infant nestled in his mother's arms. Charlie could see from the expression on her face that she really loved the baby. He felt unwanted warmth toward Antoinette Abboud, then he felt guilt and anger.

"Is your mother still around?" His voice trembled, as he felt his old fear of Antoinette Abboud.

"She'll never die. Too goddamn mean."

"She's been making calls to my mother again." He said this quietly.

Peter's eyebrows knitted in confusion. "No, Charlie, it's impossible. She hasn't been making calls to anyone, let alone your mother. She can't make calls. She's over in a nursing home nearby—'Tender Lovin' Care'—in Dearborn Heights.

She's completely out of business. She's got Parkinson's. Can't even tie her shoes. Doesn't recognize me. She never speaks."

Charlie held his head in his hands. Were the phone calls to his mother's house of shiva just a part of her imagination? Was she going as crazy as Antoinette Abboud? He looked up at Peter. "I'm sorry about your mother."

"In a weird way, I'm glad that she's this way. Now she's harmless. Does that make me a bad person?" he sighed heavily, got up from the chair, and went to the refrigerator. He pulled out a bottle of Old Bushmill's Irish whiskey. "How about something stronger to go with that beer?"

"We both could use it." Charlie turned the album page.

Peter and Georgia were posed in wedding clothes, circa 1968. He wore a Frank Zappa mustache and his hair was shoulder-length. Georgia's hair was waist-length and adorned with wildflowers. Morris Fish stood between them decked out in his favorite sharkskin suit, a proud smile on his face.

Charlie wondered what kind of lie he had cooked up to skip out on his mother to attend Peter's wedding, which was probably on a weekend. He felt anger toward his father. He thought that the days of mourning had purged him of these emotions, but he was wrong.

Peter gave him the whiskey glass. "Georgia's parents threw the wedding. It was in a big old Hungarian Catholic church in Del Ray. The reception was in this big old church basement decked out with flowers and clusters of grapes. Everybody was drunker than hell on Hungarian wine and a gypsy band played its ass off. I wish you coulda been there."

Charlie was surprised to hear that prim and proper Georgia came from a working-class ethnic background.

He turned the album page to a recent photo of Morris Fish. Pete Junior was sitting on his lap. To Charlie, seeing them together made the resemblance even more startling.

"He looks more like the old man than you or me."

"Yeah."

"They took that picture two weeks ago. It was probably his

last one." Charlie shut the album, and downed the whiskey in one gulp.

"Probably was, brother."

This was the first time that Peter had called him "brother." An electric tingle surged through his veins, like a powerful crystal meth rush. Peter was his blood kin. He felt it for the first time.

•.•

CHARLIE took Northwestern Highway back to the "Jewish suburbs," stopping off at Southfield's Lemon Tree Lounge, a dark room with piped-in Jerry Vale music. He had nothing in common with the hollow-eyed thirtyish divorcees and fast-talking polyester-clad swingers packed into the Lemon Tree; but everyone minded their own business and the drinks were cheap. He sat in a small leather booth located conveniently near the men's room. He was on his third Singapore Sling. Mixed rum drinks occasionally gave him comfort in times of great stress. All the faces from the photographs in Peter Abboud's album swirled inside his head.

He reached into his shirt pocket and pulled out his father's wallet photo accordion. He stared at the black-and-white photo of Morris Fish beaming proudly at baby Peter, his half-brother. He felt jealousy. He couldn't remember his father looking at him like that in any of the pictures that they had taken together. He couldn't remember a moment when his father was ever proud of him.

He finished the Singapore Sling. He waved at the buxom, spandex-clad, fifty-year-old cocktail waitress for a third refill. She nodded at him, a cynical expression on her face. Charlie's shabby attire eliminated any possibility of a generous tip.

∵

At 8:00 P.M., Charlie arrived at his mother's apartment. A folding TV table was set up in front of the plastic-covered, sea-foam-green couch in the living room. His Aunt Beatrice was busy placing silverware and food on the TV table. The aroma of homemade beef brisket and mashed potatoes struck his senses. Booze always made him hungry.

"Hello, Aunt Beatrice. Where's my mother?"

She looked up at him, an irritated expression on her face. "So the prodigal son returns. Where the hell have you been, Charles?"

He shook his head in frustration. "I'm tired and I'm not in the mood for a fight, Aunt Beatrice."

"You're not tired. You're high on something. While we've all been sitting shiva for your father, you've been getting loaded like a goy all week."

"No, I've been getting the truth about my father all week, while the rest of you build him up to be a saint. Pure bullshit." He turned to leave the room. "I'm going to bed."

"Don't open a mouth like that to me and walk away, young man! You should only be like your father."

"I want you to see something, Aunt Beatrice." He displayed the photo of his father and five-year-old Peter Abboud. "Take a good look." He moved closer toward her, pushing the picture at her face.

She jerked her head away from the photograph. "Get that away from me! I don't want to see it!"

"Look at it!" He shoved the photo at her, almost smacking her in the face.

"No! You go to hell! You're no damn good!" she screamed and slapped it out of his hand. The photo fell to the carpet.

He turned to face her. "My entire life I've heard you, my mother, and my father say that I'm no damn good. . . . Okay, so I'm no damn good and Morris Fish was Abraham-fucking-Lincoln!"

She began to sob. "Your father—my beloved brother—made one mistake in his life. Let him rest."

"What's going on in here?" Celia Fish wheeled her chair into the room.

Aunt Beatrice regained her composure. "Everything's fine, Celia. Go eat."

She rolled her wheelchair closer to Charlie and her sister-in-law. "There's something wrong, isn't there?" She searched their faces for any clues to their conversation. As she moved even closer, she heard the sound of one of the wheels on her chair rolling over paper. Aunt Beatrice's eyes widened in panic.

Celia glanced down, and picked up the crumpled photograph. "What's this?"

"It's nothing," stammered Beatrice as she reached for the picture. "I'll throw it in the trash."

Celia rolled toward the TV table.

Charlie gasped, as his mother set the photograph flat on the TV table and smoothed out the creases. Aunt Beatrice growled under her breath at him, "See what you did?"

Celia stared wordlessly at the photo. She blinked hard several times.

Beatrice reached for the picture. "I'll take it away, Celia!"

"Stop!" she slapped her sister-in-law's hand away. Beatrice flinched. Her face flushed deep red.

Charlie approached his mother. "He's my brother," he said gently.

She looked up, her face twisted with hatred. "You big dumb fool!" she hissed. She angrily ripped up the photo and scattered the tiny pieces onto the carpet like confetti.

"No, Celia!" sobbed Aunt Beatrice.

"You shut up!" she shrieked.

Beatrice backed away. Charlie had never seen his aunt intimidated by anyone, especially by his mother.

"Okay, my son. Now I'll give you what you want. Your father was a liar, a loser, a rat. Everything he touched turned to garbage . . . and you're exactly like him."

"No! Don't say that about him!" Aunt Beatrice cried.

"I'm say what I damn well want! This is my house! Get out, both of you!" snarled Celia.

Beatrice Sternbaum recoiled and almost knocked over a floor lamp.

Charlie held his ground. "My brother was at this apartment, mother. You met him."

"Your brother? You call that trash your brother?" Celia laughed bitterly; and aimed a hate-filled gaze at her son.

"I can't stand it," Aunt Beatrice covered her eyes with her hands and ran out of the apartment.

"He's not trash. I went to his house today, mother. I met his wife. He has children. He's a good man."

"You went to his house? You dumb idiot! Don't you remember what that beast—his mother—did to us for all those years?"

"I remember that I was eight years old and you made me answer her phone calls. You wouldn't take the phone off the hook because you were afraid of missing a call from one of your phony friends. I was eight years old! It scared the shit out of me! That's what I remember, mother. All you cared about was your goddamn friends."

"So now I'm a bad mother. You drugged-up ingrate. The doctor at the tuberculosis hospital at Herman Kiefer told me not to have you. He said giving birth to you would kill me. I should've listened to him. I should've had the abortion!" She moved the wheelchair away from him, and rolled as fast as she could toward her bedroom.

Charlie ran after her. "You're not gonna hit and run, mother! I want to talk to you!"

"Drop dead!" she screamed and slammed the bedroom door behind her.

Charlie flung open the door and entered.

"Get out!"

He ran to her and knelt down next to the chair. He moved

his face close to her, and whispered into her ear, slowly emphasizing each word, "My brother's name is Peter Abboud."

"No!" She slapped his face as hard as she could.

Charlie stood up. A red welt covered almost the entire left side of his face. He trembled with shock. This was the first time that his mother had ever hit him.

"Go to your so-called goddamn 'brother.' I want no part of you."

"Okay, mother, but before I go, I have a present for you. It's from Dad."

"What the hell are you talking about now, you screwball?"

He reached inside his shirt and pulled out the bundles of money, throwing each one at her feet.

Her mouth dropped open. "What is that?"

"There's more." He pulled bundles from his pants pockets, and threw them one by one into the pile of money at her feet. "You're rich, mother. Almost sixty-grand. Florida money."

"Where did it come from? Are you selling dope?"

"No, mother, it's Morris Fish's final act. A gift to you. He died a mensch."

"I don't believe you! You pick it all up and get it out of here!"

"Do you want to see his suicide note? I have it right here." Charlie pulled the note out of his shirt pocket. "He killed himself. Plain and simple." He thrust the note at her.

She stared at the page without reading the words. She slumped in her chair, all the fight drained out of her. "Take it away. I don't want it," she said quietly.

Charlie placed the note on top of the pile of money. "Keep the money, mother. Tell no one about it. It's a new start. Let some happiness into your life. That's what he wanted. . . . He finally did something right." He turned to leave.

She cried softly.

"I'm tired, mother. I'm going back to my place. I need sleep." Charlie bent down and lightly kissed her forehead.

He left the room.

Celia Fish slowly pulled her body out of the wheelchair. She stared down at the money, then picked up one of the bundles and fingered it.

∴

last day
of shiva

· 1976 ·

AT 10 A.M., Charlie wound up back in Dearborn. He stopped at a phone booth on Michigan Avenue. Thumbing through a weatherbeaten Yellow Pages, he found the address for the "Tender Lovin' Care" nursing home.

At a gas station, an old Lebanese man with a spinal curvature that nearly bent him in half babbled out a series of directions in pidgin English. "You go over dere, Joy Road, see Goodrich plant, then right, Top Hat hamburger, follow lef' past big big radio tower, right, Baimbridge Street, you can't miss it. Hab nice day."

Charlie eventually found Bainbridge Street and the Tender Lovin' Care nursing home, which was actually a converted tract ranch house in Briarfield Estates, a typical gone-bust subdivision from the Sixties real estate development boom. The gated driveway and high fence surrounding the ranch house were the only evidence that it was being used as a nursing home.

Charlie rang the buzzer next to the front gate. Nearly five minutes passed before there was a response; a shrill voice blurted out from the speaker next to the gate buzzer. "Yas? Who are you here for?"

"Mrs. Abboud."

"Yas?"

"I'm a friend of the family, her son Peter. My name is Charles Fish."

There was again no response for almost five minutes; then the buzzer sounded, a lip-fart. He pulled open the gate and was greeted by a stern, distinguished-looking, middle-aged black woman in a spotless starched white nurse uniform. She extended her hand for a brief professional shake. "I'm Mrs. Mills. I apologize for keeping you waiting, but we had to call Mr. Abboud for authorization. He's Mrs. Abboud's conservator. Facility policy."

Charlie followed the nurse through an oddly elegant courtyard filled with multicolored tulips and manicured hedges, a pleasant contrast to the drab subdivision ranch house. The nurse led him to a side porch door. She led him through the living room, a tastefully decorated "granny's living room" with rosebud-patterned wallpaper and homey overstuffed chairs and couches. Peter had provided well for his mother, thought Charlie. He felt a twinge of guilt, because he'd provided his own mother with nothing, not even emotional comfort.

There were only five people in the large living room. Several very elderly women and one elderly man in various stages of dementia sat up, as if they were propped up, on the couches and chairs. The man's mouth moved, his words audible only to himself. A tiny bright-eyed nurse stood in the center of the room clapping in rhythm to a disco version of "The Alleycat Dance" as an ancient frail lady shuffle-stepped and rattled a tambourine. "Good girl, Dora! Thataway!" the tiny nurse chirped gleefully.

Charlie felt deep sadness. He could imagine his own mother becoming a dependent drugged-out zombie like this bunch. He followed Mrs. Mills down a hallway. "Mrs. Abboud is a bit under the weather today. She's in her room."

The nurse led him to a bedroom that was larger than his entire apartment. Charlie recognized some of the furniture that he had seen in Antoinette Abboud's living room from the picture window in the Highland Park house. That living room was forever engrained in his memory. He shuddered, then gasped at the sight of Antoinette Abboud.

She lay in the massive bed that dominated the room. Her body formed a stiff letter-W shape. Her right hand trembled uncontrollably with a life of its own. Although she couldn't have been older than sixty, Antoinette Abboud had been transformed into a sick old lady, an eighty-pound skeletal creature. Her raven-black hair had turned fright-wig white. Her face sunk in at the mouth.

He couldn't believe that this was the same woman who had terrorized his family years ago. Only her long scarlet manicured fingernails indicated the vain flamboyant dangerous person that she once was. "She has Parkinson's Disease," Mrs. Mills said in a hush. "The last stage. She may not recognize you, Mr. Fish. She also has dementia."

Charlie felt faint. He steadied himself and cautiously approached the bed.

"You can't stay too long, Mr. Fish."

"I know."

Mrs. Mills smiled, nodded politely, and left the room.

He squatted on his haunches next to her. Her scent was a combination of antiseptic and urine. His stomach churned. He moved his face close to her ear. Her gaze appeared to be focused on a point on the ceiling. "Do you know who I am?" he said quietly.

Her eyelids blinked several times, but she still focused on the ceiling. Charlie interpreted this as a response.

"I'm Charlie Fish, Morris's son."

She turned her head toward him, and stared straight into his eyes. He felt a chill of fear. "I know you," she said. Her voice was a bullfrog's croak. Her face twisted into a toothless smile. She began to laugh, a harsh whispering laugh.

Charlie jerked away from her. He remembered the sound of her laughter, the same maniacal telephone laughter that he had heard as a boy. For a moment, he forgot that she was a frail pitiful old lady twitching helplessly in a sick room bed.

He choked down his hatred. "I just met my brother—your son—Peter."

Her derisive smile changed to a witch's scowl. "Your brother?" she said these two words slowly. "*Your* brother?" she repeated these words louder. Her mouth opened wide, forming a dark rathole. A shrieking cackle emerged.

"He's not your brother, Jewboy! Not my Peter!"

Charlie lurched away from her, almost falling over. His head throbbed with shooting pains. He trembled uncontrollably, as if he had caught her Parkinson's Disease.

He placed his palms flat on the carpet to steady himself. He tried to calm his racing mind. He tried to remember that she had dementia, that she was probably raving mad.

She stopped laughing. Her scowl vanished. She stared at him for several moments without expression. She smiled. It was almost a kindly smile. "Don't be afraid. Come close." Her voice was gentle, grandmotherly.

He gathered his courage and moved toward her, his face only inches away from her lips. Her breath smelled like bile. "Do you really believe that my Peter is your brother?"

"Yes."

She snatched his shirt collar in her bony hand and jerked him closer, his ear touching her slobbering mouth. "Do you want to know the truth, Jewboy?"

He tried to pull away, but she had a death-grip on his collar.

"Listen to me, Charlie Fish. Morris was nothin' but a goddamn sucker. I took him an' the rest of them Jew suckers for plenty!" Her cackle nearly pierced his eardrum as he pulled himself away from her.

She propped herself up on bony elbows, like Lazarus coming back to life. "Whatsamatter, Jewboy? Are you afraid of me? Are you afraid of the truth?" Her eyes glistened with hatred.

"I'm not afraid of you." Charlie glared back at her.

"Peter isn't your brother. Your old man was shootin' blanks. Couldn't cut the mustard. Peter is Lowell Krantz's bastard." Her mouth twisted into a smug smile.

Charlie opened his mouth, trying to catch his breath.

"You know Mr. Rich Big Shot Lowell Krantz, don'tcha, Jewboy? Well, I took him just like your old man," she chortled. "Yeah, they say that Jews are smart about money. Well, bullshit. They're like everybody else when it comes to their prick."

Her shrieks of laughter tore through him. He tried to scramble to his feet and fell to the floor face-first. He pulled himself up to his knees. A stream of blood ran from his nostril.

"Whatsamatter, little Jewboy? You can't take it?" she shrieked.

He rose to his feet. The impact of the fall had made him woozy. He planted himself firmly in the carpet and pointed a quavering finger at her. "Peter is my brother, Antoinette. I don't care what you say. He'll always be my brother."

Her laughter grew even louder. "You're an even bigger sucker than your old man, if that's possible!"

Charlie clamped his hands over his ears. He could take no more of her. He rushed out of the bedroom. He pushed past two nurses running down the hall, alarmed at the sounds of Antoinette Abboud's crazed gales of laughter.

He could still hear her screams as he fled the building. "Sucker!"

∴

CHARLIE parked his car in the Workmen's Circle cemetery parking lot. Except for a groundskeeper truck, the lot was empty. He figured that he was probably the only visitor there. He flung open the car door and stumbled out. His eyes were red and swollen. Bloody snot crusted in his mustache. He had cried all the way from the nursing home in Dearborn Heights to the cemetery in Mount Clemens.

He tried to remember where his father was buried. He pushed his way through the jumble of old headstones and weeds. There would be no tombstone placed on his father's grave until a year after burial, a Jewish tradition called "unveiling." This made his search more difficult. He remembered seeing a name on a nearby headstone during his father's burial: "Julius Marx." This was Groucho's real name. Groucho was his favorite comedian. The "Julius Marx" in the old photo embedded in the tombstone looked nothing like Groucho Marx. The tombstone-Julius-Marx was a thin Hassidic Jew with a black beard.

Charlie searched for almost a half an hour. He had an almost blinding headache. He stopped every few feet to lean against a tall grave marker.

He found "Julius Marx's" headstone and Morris Fish's gravesite. Tiny blades of grass were beginning to sprout from the small hill of dirt. Charlie sat down next to his father's grave.

"Hi, dad. I thought I lost you." He realized the irony of his words. He smiled briefly, then felt a deep anguish.

Charlie burst into tears. He dug his fingers into the earth, gritted his jaws, and forced himself to stop crying.

"What the fuck am I doing? I'm in a graveyard talking to myself. I gotta be nuts." He started laughing. He reclined in

a spread-eagle position on top of the grave. "You're dead.
I'm nuts. And there's nothing anybody can do about it."

He laughed loudly. "She called you a sucker, dad. My
mother calls you a saint. A Jewish saint. Who's lying? Who
cares?"

He shut his eyes. "I met Peter, dad. It doesn't matter
whether he's your son and my brother. I don't care. You were
right. He is a good man. A mensch. And so am I. I came here
to say goodbye the right way, dad, not the Jewish way, not
mother's way."

Charlie tasted the salty bitterness of his tears. He config-
ured his body into a fetal position.

"Dad, I came to tell you that I'm leaving. Putting the past
in the past. Detroit is the past. You're the past. So is mother
and Antoinette Abboud. I love you, but I can't wind up
trapped like you. I have to leave the past to know myself."
He sat up abruptly.

Charlie took his wallet out of his pocket, thumbed
through the ten hundred-dollar bills, his father's gift, and
found the old photo of his family at Knotts Berry Farm. As
he stared at the yellowing photo, he felt deep sadness. "Your
dream was to live in California, dad. You never did, and you
regretted it your entire life. All you had to do was pack all
your shit, shove mother and me into the car, and go. Just as
simple as that. Or maybe it wasn't so simple for you. It's simple for me. It's goddamn simple."

Charlie gently placed the photo on the grave, then stood
up. "Goodbye, dad. You did the best you could," he said
quietly.

He thrashed his way past the tombstones and weeds, leaving Workmen's Circle Cemetery behind.

∴

Charlie's Bumblebee drove down the expressway, passing a Toledo exit. He had no idea if the Bumblebee would survive the long haul west. If not, he'd take a Greyhound bus the rest of the way.

He placed Howieschultz's business card on top of the dashboard.

He tried to memorize Howie's Los Angeles phone number. He repeated it in his head.

"213-822-9202."

∴